Praise for Laurence Shames

MANGROVE SQUEEZE
'Like Elmore Leonard, Shames mixes comedy and crime expertly
. . . A delightfully offbeat crime comedy, Florida style' *Booklist*

'Critics have compared Shames to the great crime absurdist Carl
Hiaasen, but he's not only treading on the master's heels; in plot,
invention, and sheer vigour he's overtaken him' *Literary Review*

VIRGIN HEAT
'This slapstick caper, a gravity-defying structure of impossible
coincidences, has been built for fun. Even his zaniest characters
have a dark core that gives them dimension in this sun-bleached
land of forgetting' *New York Times Book Review*

TROPICAL DEPRESSION
'Like Charles Willeford, Elmore Leonard and Carl Hiaasen, Laurence Shames is a specialist in tales of low and high jinks in humid
places' *San Francisco Chronicle*

SUNBURN
'From the first page to the last, *Sunburn* charms' *Miami Herald*

SCAVENGER REEF
'A mix of hilarity and menace saturated with a physical sense of
Key West . . . Superior entertainment' *New York Times*

FLORIDA STRAITS
'Mr. Shames turns out characters flashier than a Key West sunset
and dialogue tastier than a conch stew' *New York Times Book
Review*

LAURENCE SHAMES

Welcome to Paradise

ORION

This edition published in Great Britain
in 1999 by Orion
An imprint of Orion Books Ltd
Orion House, 5 Upper St Martin's Lane,
London WC2H 9EA

A CIP catalogue record for this book
is available from the British Library

Printed and bound in Great Britain by
Clays Ltd, St Ives plc

To Marilyn,
who laughs,
with love

PROLOGUE

"Was the clams," said Nicky Scotto.

"Ya sure?" said Donnie Falcone. Skeptically, he tugged on a long and fleshy earlobe. "Ya sure it was the clams?"

"Hadda be the clams." Nicky sipped anisette and looked vaguely toward the window of Nono's Pasticceria. Nono's was on Carmine Street, two steps below the sidewalk. Half a century of exhaust fumes had tinted its front window a restful bluish gray. People talked softly in Nono's. Never loud enough to be heard above the steaming of the milk. Nicky put his glass down, said, "Fuck else could it'a been?"

Carefully, fastidiously, Donnie broke a *biscotto,* herded up crumbs with the flat of his thumb. He hated when crumbs got stuck in the fibers of his big black overcoat. "How should I know? What else j'eat?"

Nicky winced just slightly and softly belched at the recollection of the catastrophic meal. He pictured the breadsticks, the drops of wine on the tablecloth. His fist still pressed against his lips, he said, "Minestrone."

"Minestrone," echoed Donnie. "Ya don't puke off minestrone."

"Hadda be the clams," Nicky said once more. He leaned back in the booth, smoothed the creamy mohair of his jacket. Dark and thickly built, he was handsome until you looked a little closer. The jaw was square but just a little heavy, the black eyes too close to the thick and slightly piggish nose.

Donnie kept his eyes down on his pastry plate. "Ya sure you're not just lookin' for a reason to get mad at Al?"

When Nicky was agitated, his voice got softer instead of louder. His throat squeezed down like a crimped hose and words came out with the razzing purr of a muted trumpet. "I don't need another fuckin' reason to be mad at Al."

Donnie thought it best to leave it right there. "Okay. What else j'eat?"

Nicky absently ran fingertips against the wall. The wall was covered with small white tiles, broken up with ranks of gold and black at shoulder level. "Broccoli rabe," he said. "Scallopini veal, lemon sauce. Some pasta shit, little hats, like."

Donnie said, "Orecchiette?"

"Fuck knows?" said Nicky. "Look, I didn't come here to discuss macaroni shapes, okay? I come here to tell ya what that fuck Al did to me."

"A few bad clams," said Donnie. "Happens."

"Look, when I had the fish market, I did the right thing. I didn't give bad clams to places where friends of ours was gonna eat."

"Nicky. How is Al supposed to know you're gonna be eatin' in some hotel up inna Catskills?"

The question slowed Nicky down. His fingernails tickled the grout between the tiles.

Donnie went on. "Truth, Nicky, I don't see you inna fuckin' Catskills either. It's a Jew place."

"Used ta be," said Nicky. "Now it's everything. Hotels for queers. For Puerto Ricans. Couple good Italian places, you know that."

"Okay, okay. But whaddya do up there? Play shuffleboard?"

Embarrassed, Nicky said, "Ya look at leaves."

"Leaves?"

"I tol' ya, Donnie," Nicky said. "My mother-in-law, it was her seventieth. My wife says, 'She loves the autumn. Let's take her to the leaves.' So I say okay. The old broad wantsta look at leaves, I'm tryin' to be nice. Wha' could I tell ya—this is who I am."

Donnie drained his espresso, motioned for another. From behind his arm, he said, "It ain't the clams. You're mad 'cause Tony Eggs took the fish away from you and gave it to Big Al."

Nicky tugged at the collar of his turtleneck, twisted his head around in a circle. "'Course I'm mad," he finally admitted. "Fuck wit' a man's livelihood, who ain't gonna be mad?" There was a silence, and when the stocky man spoke again he could not quite hide a real sorrow and bewilderment. "Why'd he do it, Donnie?"

Donnie shrugged. He had a long thin face and a long thin neck, and when he shrugged, his shoulders had a lot of ground to cover. His skin had a grayish-yellow cast and his usual expression was distantly amused yet mournful. "I ain't got a clue."

"Come on—the man's your uncle."

"Great-uncle," corrected Donnie, and came close to revealing some pique of his own. "An' ya see how close we are. Me, I'm still hustling window-cleaning contracts inna fuckin' garment district."

Nicky made a vague and universal griping sound.

Donnie sipped coffee and quietly went on. "Look, the market's Big Al's now. Ya gotta let it go."

"This ain't about the market."

"I wish I could believe that."

"What this is about is that he poisoned me. Poisoned alla us."

Donnie's flat lips stretched out and came close to smiling. He wiped his mouth instead. "The t'ree a you in that hotel room—"

"Suite. It was a suite. Two bedrooms. Two bat'rooms. I thought two would be enough."

There was a pause. Outside on Carmine Street, taxis went by, the clatter of trucks filtered in from Seventh Avenue. The milk steamer hissed and Nicky got madder. Revolted. Humiliated. "Well," he went on, "two bat'rooms wasn't enough. The wife, the old lady—disgusting. Dignity? Tell me about dignity when you're leakin' both ends, hoppin' to the toilet wit' your pj's down your ankles. When your wife has to crawl over ya to get to the bowl."

"Nicky, it was just bad luck. Coulda happened to any—"

But Nicky was not to be hushed. Air wheezed through his pinched windpipe. "Ol' lady ends up whaddyacallit, intravenous. Happy birt'day, Ma. Camille, skinny marink ta begin wit', she drops six pounds. Me, I ain't right for a week. A week, Donnie! Cramps, runs, white shit on my tongue. Taste in my mouth like somethin' died. I tell ya, Donnie, a week a hell."

Donnie had settled back in the booth, all but disappearing into his coat. When Nicky finished, he leaned forward, folded his long neat hands in front of him, and said very softly, "But, Nicky, why stay mad? I mean, where we goin' wit' this? Ya gonna ice a guy over some funky seafood?"

Nicky sipped his anisette. His face went innocent. "Who said anything about icin' anyone? You said that. Not me."

"I only said—"

"Look, I'm a guy that does the right thing—"

"You keep sayin' that," Donnie pointed out.

"—and all I want is that that fuckin' guy should suffer like I suffered. A week a total misery. Justice. That's all I want. Zat too fuckin' much t'ask?"

"Justice? Yeah," said Donnie. He blotted up some crumbs. "So whaddya want from me?"

"Help. Advice. Like, ways to ruin his life."

"Nicky, I don't want no part a this. Besides, it's gonna have to wait."

"What has to wait? Wait for what?"

"Big Al's goin' outa town I heard. Goin' on vacation."

Nicky rubbed his chin. "Hey, I was on vacation too. A guy can't be mizzable on vacation?" He paused. He brightened slightly and his small black eyes squeezed down. "Where's he goin' on vacation?"

"Flahda," Donnie said reluctantly. "Key West is what I heard."

"Flahda," Nicky intoned. He drained his anisette, wrapped hot hands around the glass. He lifted up one curly eyebrow. "Flahda. Far away. That's nice. That's like the best advice you coulda gimme."

"Hey—"

"Flahda. Vacation. Far away from everything."

"You never heard it from me," said Donnie.

Nicky said, "So happens I got friends in Flahda."

ONE

1

"Why we gotta drive?" said Katy Sansone, who was twenty-nine years old and Big Al Marracotta's girlfriend.

She was bustling around the pink apartment that Big Al kept for her in Murray Hill. It was not a great apartment, but Katy, though she had her good points, was not that great a girlfriend. She complained a lot. She went right to the edge of seeming ungrateful. She had opinions and didn't seem to understand that if she refreshed her lipstick more, and answered back less, she might have had the one-bedroom with the courtyard view rather than the noisy, streetside studio with the munchkin-sized appliances. Now she was packing, roughly, showing a certain disrespect for the tiny bathing suits and thong panties and G-strings and underwire bras that Big Al had bought her for the trip.

"We have to drive," he said, "because the style in which I travel, airports have signs calling it an act of terrorism."

"Always with the guns," she pouted. "Even on vacation?"

"Several," said Big Al. "A small one for the glove compartment. A big one under the driver's seat. A fuckin' bazooka inna trunk." He smiled. "Oh, yeah—and don't forget the big knife inna sock." He was almost cute when he smiled. He had a small gap between his two front teeth, and the waxy crinkles at the corners of his eyes suggested a boyish zest. When he smiled his forehead shifted and moved the short salt-and-pepper hair that other times looked painted on. Big Al was five foot two and weighed

3

one hundred sixteen pounds. "Besides," he added, "I wanna bring the dog."

"The daw-awg!" moaned Katy.

Big Al raised a warning finger, but even before he did so, Katy understood that she should go no further. Certain things were sacred, and she could not complain about the dog. Its name was Ripper. It was a champion rottweiler and a total coward. It had coy brown eyebrows and a brown blaze on its square black head, and it dribbled constantly through the flubbery pink lips that imperfectly covered its mock-ferocious teeth. A stub of amputated tail stuck out above its brown-splashed butt, and its testicles, the right one always lower than the left, hung down and bounced as though they were on bungees. It was those showy and ridiculous nuts, she secretly believed, that made Al dote so on the dog.

She kept packing. High-heeled sandals. Open-toed pumps. Making chitchat, trying to sound neutral, she said, "So the dog's already in the car?"

Big Al nodded. "Guarding it." Again he smiled. Say this for him: he knew what gave him pleasure. He had a huge dog gnawing on a huge bone in the backseat of his huge gray Lincoln. He had a young girlfriend packing slinky things for a weeklong Florida vacation—a week of sun, sweat, sex, and lack of aggravation. For the moment he was a happy guy.

Katy snapped her suitcase closed and straightened out her back. She was five foot eleven, and Al had told her never to insult him by wearing flats. Standing there in heels and peg-leg pants, she looked a little like a missile taking off. Long lean shanks and narrow hips provided thrust that seemed to lift the dual-coned payload of chest, which tapered in turn to a pretty though small-featured face capped by a pouf of raven hair.

For a moment she just stood there by her suitcase, waiting to see if Al would pick it up. Then she picked it up herself and they headed for the door.

His face was on her bosom the whole elevator ride down to the garage. Vacation had begun.

Across the river in suburban Jersey, on the vast and cluttered selling floor of Kleiman Brothers Furniture on Route 22 in Springfield, a ceremony was in progress.

Moe Kleiman, the last survivor of the founding brothers, had taken off his shoes and was standing, somewhat shakily, on an ottoman. He stroked his pencil mustache, fiddled with the opal tie tack that, every day for many years, he'd painstakingly poked through the selfsame holes in the selfsame ties, and gestured for quiet. Benignly, he looked out across the group that he proudly referred to as the finest sales staff in the Tri-State area. For a moment he gazed beyond them to the store he loved: lamps with orange price tags hanging from their covered shades; ghostly conversation nooks in which a rocker seemed to be conferring with a La-Z-Boy; ranks of mattresses close-packed as cots in a battlefield hospital.

Then he said, "Friends, we are gathered today to announce the winner of the semi-annual bonus giveaway for top sales in dinettes."

He gestured for quiet as though there'd been applause. But the fact was that, for all of Moe Kleiman's attempts to bring some pomp to the moment, there was no suspense. Everybody knew who'd won. Who won was who almost always won. It was a regular routine already.

Nevertheless, Moe Kleiman soldiered on. "The prize this time around is the best ever. It better be. We got a fancy new travel agent and we're paying through the nose."

At this, people could not help flicking their eyes toward Alan Tuschman, the guy who always won. Twenty years before, he'd been a big-deal high school athlete—split end on the Cranford football team, power forward on a hoops squad that made it to the state semis—and, in a circumscribed, suburban way, he'd been winning ever since, sort of. Got a scholarship to Rutgers. Married a cheerleader with blond hair and amazing calves, cut and sculpted from years of leaping. The marriage didn't last; the scholarship evaporated when the coaches realized that Al Tuschman's talents wouldn't carry him beyond JV. Still, a few semesters of college and matrimony felt right while they endured, lived on in memory like bonus chapters appended to the high school yearbook.

Those temporary victories had helped to keep alive in Al the mysterious habit of winning, and he still got pumped and rallied at almost anything that could be called a game. Sales contests, for starters. Already this year he'd won the giant television set, for bedding; the trip by train to Montreal, for living rooms. His colleagues, of course, were sick of him winning, but they couldn't really find it in their hearts to resent him. He was a nice guy. Friendly. Fair. He didn't hog the floor, he didn't show off, and he didn't try too hard. People just liked to buy from him.

"The prize this time," Moe Kleiman went on, "is nothing short of Paradise. . . . Paradise—that's the name of the hotel. In Key West, Florida. Seven days, six nights. Airfare included. And the winner is—"

The old ham paused, of course. And in the pause, Alan Tuschman's fellow salesmen tried to figure out, for the thousandth time, the key to his success. Some people thought it was his height, pure and simple. At six-three and change, he was by far the tallest guy on the floor, and people felt good dealing with a tall guy. Others thought it was his looks. Not that he was model material. His cheeks were slightly pitted, his lips thick and loose; but his eyes were big and dark, the features widely spaced: it was a face that gave you room to breathe. Then there was the way he dressed—a strange amalgam of old-time collegiate jock and working-man suburban slick. Cotton cardigans over open-collared patterned shirts; pegged and shiny pants leading down to desert boots; a pinky ring that clattered up against a chunky school memento, class of '77. In its careless inconsistency, Al's style gave almost everyone something to hang on to.

"And the winner is," Moe Kleiman said again, "Alan Tuschman."

Amid thin and brief applause that was swallowed up by mattresses and chair backs, someone said, "Surprise!"

"Alan Tuschman," Moe went on, "who in the past six months, *in dinettes alone,* wrote a hundred twenty-eight thousand dollars' worth of business. Ladies and gentleman, that is selling! . . . Al, have a well-earned rest in Paradise!"

The boss shook Al Tuschman's hand, discreetly used the clasp as an aid in stepping off the ottoman.

A couple of colleagues slapped Al's back, and then the group dispersed, spread out through the beds and the imaginary living rooms to the four corners of the premises. It was 9:55 and the store opened at ten. Every day. No matter what.

By a quarter of eleven, thinking of vacation, Al had sold a French provincial love seat and a wall unit made to look like rosewood. But then he grew troubled, and stepped around the low wall of frosted glass that separated the sales floor from the offices. He poked his head into Moe Kleiman's tidy cubicle. "Mr. Kleiman," he said, "I have a problem with this prize."

The boss lifted his head and raised an eyebrow. When he did that he looked a great deal like the old guy from Monopoly.

"If it's all the same to you," said Al, "I'm not gonna use the plane ticket."

"All of a sudden you don't fly?" Moe Kleiman said.

Al Tuschman looked a little bit sheepish. "Truth is, it's the dog."

"The dog?"

"Remember last year, I won that package to New Orleans?"

"I remember, I remember."

"The dog was, like, traumatic. Put her in the carrier, she looked at me like I was sending her to the gas chamber. Then the

7

tranquilizers made her sick. Woke up shaking. Laid down on my shoe so I wouldn't go anywhere. Two days I stayed in the hotel, looking out the window with this shell-shocked dog on my foot. I couldn't put her through that again. I'll drive. That okay with you?"

"Sure, Al. Sure. Only, the reservation starts tomorrow."

"You don't mind, I could leave today."

Moe Kleiman stood up, took a token glance out toward the selling floor. A Tuesday in the first half of November. Very quiet. He said, "No problem, Al. If it makes things easier for the dog."

"Thanks," said Tuschman. "Thanks for everything. You'll see, I'll come back tan and sell my ass off."

He turned to go. He was not yet forty, but these days, when he pivoted, he felt old tackles in his knees; the small bones in his ankles remembered rebounds when he didn't land quite right.

He was just rounding the wall of frosted glass when he heard Moe Kleiman chuckle. "The dog. Hey, Al, ya know something?"

The salesman took a step back toward his boss.

The boss lowered his voice. "The other guys, it drives them nuts, they constantly wonder why you're always top banana. But I know. I could give it to you in a word."

Al Tuschman did not ask what the word was. He didn't want to know. Like everybody else, he had his superstitious side. Something worked, you didn't jinx it.

Moe Kleiman told him anyway. "Relief."

"Relief?"

"Relief. People see you, Al—big shoulders, chest hair up to the Adam's apple—they figure, Oy, I'm dealing with a tough guy. Their guard goes up. But it soon comes down, and then you've got 'em. Why does it come down? I'll tell you: because they're relieved to see you really are a softie."

Pleased with his analysis, Moe Kleiman smiled.

Al Tuschman tried to, but it didn't work. His mouth slid to one side of his face; he looked down at a swatch book, shuffled his feet. A softie. Softie as in pushover? As in coward? Was it really that obvious? Did everybody know? He briefly met his boss's gaze, made another bent attempt at smiling, and steered his aching legs toward the partition.

Moe Kleiman watched his best salesman edge around the frosted glass, and understood too late that he'd barged in on a secret, that he should have kept his mouth shut. A note of pleading in his voice, he said, "Al, hey, I meant it as a compliment."

2

"*But, Nicky,*" *said* Charlie "Chop" Parilla, "I don't even know the guy."

"Perfect."

"Perfect? What perfect? Hol' on a minute." He pressed the phone against his hairy, sweating stomach and screamed across the garage at the two workmen who were using giant hammers to bang the doors off a brand-new BMW 740i. "Ya see I'm onna phone. Try a fuckin' wrench." He dried the receiver on his pants leg, put it back against his ear. "What's perfect, I don't know the guy?"

"Motive, Chop," said Nicky Scotto. He was calling from a pay phone down on Broome Street. It was starting to snow. Two weeks before Thanksgiving, and thin, defective snow like a confetti of waxed paper was already blowing sideways through the street. "Ya don't know the guy, ya got no reason to torment 'im. No one's gonna suspect."

Chop Parilla scratched his ample belly, flicked moisture from his fingers. In Hialeah it was eighty-six and muggy. The doors of the garage were closed. Had to be when you were doing unrequested autopsies on other people's cars. Lifting engines out like guts. Scalpeling away spare parts until sometimes nothing but the drive train sat there on the lift, forlorn as the excised backbone of a chicken. "I don't know. Sounds like trouble."

"Trouble?" said Nicky. Wet snow was tickling his Adam's

apple and putting evanescent sparkles in his hair. "Think of it as fun. Twenty grand for a week a trailin' someone you don't care about one way or the other, and fuckin' wit' his head."

Chop watched as the wheels were lifted off the Beemer. Very handsome wheels. Aircraft-grade aluminum. He said, "If this guy's a big cheese in New York . . . I don't know what you're puttin' me inna middle of."

"There is no middle," Nicky said. "This is strictly unofficial. A small, personal matter . . . Look, Chop, I know the fuckin' shithole where you work. Wouldn't you like a paid excuse to get outa there awhile?"

Parilla thought that over. It was true that Hialeah got depressing. All those sunburned beggars with signs around their necks, sitting at intersections clogged with smoking cars blasting "murder-Castro" call-in shows. But on the other hand, in Hialeah Chop was doing what he was put on earth to do. Stealing cars. Taking them apart. Sometimes putting them together again in changed configurations. Gaskets; fuel injectors; the snaking cables of clutches. He loved them all; they spoke to him. If a couple of breaks had fallen differently, he might have ended up a smiling, legit mechanic with a computerized wheel-alignment gizmo and his name embroidered on his pocket, a regular Mr. Goodwrench.

Nicky Scotto broke into his reverie. "Go down to the Keys? Sunsets. Margaritas. A little poontang, maybe?"

This made it pretty tempting. But there were problems. "Nicky, how I even find this guy?"

On the snowy New York corner, Nicky Scotto smiled. "Easy."

"Easy for you to say easy."

"He's a little guy wit' a big dog—"

"Oh, great," said Chop. "That really narrows it—"

"—and a vanity plate."

"Vanity plate?" said Chop. "The asshole's got a vanity plate?"

"Did I tell ya he's a putz or what? Tells all the world, BIG AL."

Chop Parilla shook his head. It was a small head on a large

body. At the back, neck became skull in one straight line; in front, the jaw barely lifted clear of the collarbones—it looked like he'd have to jack his chin up to shave beneath it. Vanity plate. "Make it thirty grand, I'll do it."

"Thirty," said Nicky. "Now you're gettin' greedy."

"No," said Chop. "In fact I'm takin' a cut. Ya want this job done like it oughta be, I need a second guy."

On Broome Street the snow was getting drier. Nicky brushed flakes of it from the lapel of his camel-hair topcoat. "Have someone in mind?"

The guys in the garage had started hammering again. In syncopation with the tapping, Chop said, "Only the perfect guy for this job. Sid the Squid."

Nicky Scotto smiled, narrowing his piggish eyes. Snowflakes tickled his gums. Squid Berman. Nicky knew him by reputation only. But what a reputation. A warped, perverted, morbid, and sickly artful madman; perhaps a genius. "But wait," he said. "I thought I heard that Squid was inna slammer. Heisting a racehorse or something."

"Not a racehorse. Couple greyhounds. Got caught red-handed with a can of Alpo. But that was like three hitches ago. He just got out again."

"Wha'd they get 'im for this time?"

"Stealing letters," Chop Parilla said.

"Letters? Squid? That's stupid. Federal."

"Not letters," said Chop. "*Letters*. Big, gigantic letters offa hotel signs. Ya know, South Beach, deco. Wanted to make a huge, gigantic billboard that said YOU TOO."

"You too?"

"Don't ask me," said Chop. "He got it in his head. Anyway, he could use some dough and he could use some entertainment."

"Squid Berman," Nicky said with satisfaction. Why hadn't he thought of him himself? "Okay, Chop. Bring 'im in, ya got your thirty grand."

•

Big Al Marracotta spent that night in a Holiday Inn near San-
tee, South Carolina. By the time he drove across the Florida line
next day, Ripper's rawhide bone had been masticated into a
gooey mess, the Jerry Vale and Al Martino tapes had been listened to so many times that even the harp parts had trickled into
memory, and Katy Sansone was nowhere to be seen. Her face finally came up from underneath the steering wheel somewhere
north of Cocoa Beach.

Around Daytona, polishing her toenails, which rested on the
glove box with the little gun inside, she said, "I hate long car
trips."

"Relaxing," said Big Al. He gestured left and right. "Look at
the palm trees."

"I'd rather watch the license plates," she said. "Michigan. Ontario."

Alan Tuschman, meanwhile, was lagging a state or so behind,
driving a cruise-control seventy in his leased silver Lexus, and
mostly talking to his dog, Fifi.

"Feef," he said, scratching her behind the ears, "dogs have it
pretty good. You realize that?"

The dog luxuriously lolled her head from side to side, blithely
entrusting her knobby little skull to her master's enormous
hand. She was a shih tzu with an attitude, immaculately
groomed and wholly the coquette. Arching bangs lent mystery to
her black and glassy eyes. Her small pink tongue, not much
wider than an anchovy, was an organ of flirtation. Her walk was
proud and bouncy—a cheerleader's walk; she had a way of looking back across her shoulder that created a distinct impression of
Bacall. But for all her apparent frippery, she had reserves of
steadfastness and courage that had never yet been tested, but
simmered at the ready nonetheless. Now, at ease and intimate,
she lay on her back and let herself be stroked.

"You're a dog," said Al, "people don't expect that much. Don't gotta be strong just because you're big. Don't gotta keep winning the same game over and over again. What ya gotta do? Not pee on the floor. Roll over. Sit down, ya wanna biscuit. 'Course, ya gotta be loyal."

He stopped petting her just long enough to wag an index finger in her face. She licked the finger then bit down lightly on the bulbous knuckle.

"Loyalty's big," he went on. "Then again, it's big in people too. But somehow it's more appreciated in a dog. . . . And look at the other advantages. Say it's the middle of the afternoon and you wanna go to bed. You curl up with a rubber hamburger and people say how cute. None of this wondering am I depressed, is something wrong? . . . Or even, like, with sex. You're young, you have a fling or two, a good screaming hump across a couple of backyards, then boom, ya get fixed and your worries are over. None of this wondering do I still look good, am I hip, if I get somebody in the sack with me, how's it gonna go? I don't see where being a dog is such a bad deal."

Fifi did nothing to change his mind. She scratched her supple back against the leather upholstery, kicked her manicured and carefree paws into the air.

Al Tuschman stretched his dully aching legs and let out a deep, unhurried sigh that filled the car. He was thinking something that he wouldn't say aloud, even to the dog.

He was thinking how odd it was to have worked so hard to win this contest, to have *had* to win this contest, when the truth was that he needed a trip to Florida like he needed a hole in the head. Oh, the sun would be nice. He'd enjoy people's envy of his tan. It would feel good to dunk in a pool, and maybe he'd get lucky in the bars. But he couldn't help believing, secretly, that all in all he'd be happier at home. In his neighborhood. In the store. Where he knew what he was doing and who he was.

On vacation, who was he? One more aimless, nameless shmeggegi in boxer trunks, getting a headache from drinking in the afternoon sun, desperately pretending to be loving every minute. A disconnected guy waiting for life to throw him an experience.

Whereas at home he was comfortable, recognized, embraced. A well-liked character who got warm hellos in diners. Who kibitzed with the car-wash guys, the cops. Everybody knew him, or as much of him as he wanted them to. Maybe as much of him as he knew himself. The schoolboy hero. The top salesman. The smiling, easy fella who'd started putting up big numbers at an early age, and was putting them up still. The kind of guy who had a nickname known even to people who hadn't actually met him.

Big Al. Slightly famous in his town, a legend in his neighborhood.

3

There is one road leading to Key West.

Like a muddy river draining many streams, U.S. 1 gathers up the suckers who feed the resort economy, and the seekers who refresh the town's battered and eroding soul, and funnels them into two thin lanes that hop from key to key between the ocean and the Gulf, between ranks of power lines and strings of pelicans, between dank motels and stalking egrets, salty bars and patient barracuda, porno stores and sweeping tides. There are exits from this road but they are all dead ends, incomplete, unsatisfying stoppings-short. Only one route leads through to the edge that is powerfully agreed upon as the finish to this part of the world. On that hurtling and constricted path there is nowhere to hide.

Which is why Chop Parilla and Squid Berman had positioned themselves on the shoulder of the highway just where it crosses Cow Key Bridge and enters Key West proper.

It was early afternoon when they took up their post. The sun drew steam out of the mangroves when it broke between the spongy clouds that were blowing westward, carrying with them some of the last of the prodigious summer rains. The day grew hotter and traffic rumbled on the bridge. Each sort of vehicle made a different noise. Mopeds buzzed like paper on a comb. Cars plunked over seams in the concrete. Trucks forced a groan from the trestles and sent forth walls of wind that whistled in the railings.

Sid the Squid, morbidly sensitive to noises, as to most things, was made jumpy by the cacophony. He kept getting out of Chop Parilla's Jaguar—a mosaic of extracted, reassembled parts—patrolling some yards of Florida, and climbing in again.

Squid was built to be jumpy. He was shorter than average, and small-boned, but with incongruously bandy muscles that swelled between his narrow joints; at moments it seemed like he might snap his arms and legs from movements too spasmodic. His elbows were pointy, like Popeye's, and his Adam's apple stuck out so far that it deformed the collars of his T-shirts. His eyeballs bulged, and an improbable expanse of white could usually be seen around his flickering hazel irises. Now he dove back into the idling, air-conditioned Jag and said, "Hey, Chop, y'ever do a job like this before?"

"No." Truth was, Parilla's career had cleaved to the mundane. Besides stealing cars, he collected loans, occasionally set insurance fires, broke fingers and noses when it was unavoidable. Straightforward stuff, conventional.

"Me neither," said the Squid. "But I like it. I'm psyched. Ya know what I like about it, Chop?"

He paused what was, for him, a beat, but for most other people was a quarter beat. Chop did not have time to answer, and Squid went on in his chronically humid voice, the voice of someone with too much wetness seeping through the blue strands underneath his tongue.

"It makes no sense. I mean, it's pure—it has no purpose. Not like, say, robbing something. Torching something. Vulgar ordinary shit. Where's the creativity in that? This is like . . . it's like getting paid to be a gremlin. Hired to direct a nightmare. Yeah! Ya see what I'm sayin'?"

The statement was a little high-flown and abstract for Chop. He answered, "Can we steal his car?"

Squid rolled his bulging eyes. "That ain't the job."

"We're s'posed t'annoy him," argued Chop. "Wouldn't that annoy him?"

Squid didn't answer. He sprang out of the Jag again, paced along the shoulder, listening to the orchestra of traffic.

Shadows started to lengthen, silhouettes of palms were pasted on the roadway. The sun went from white to yellow and revealed the fine grain of the inconstant air. After a time Chop lowered the electric window and yelled out, "Squid, let's get a cuppa coffee."

The bandy man hesitated. He was launched on a performance, bringing to bear on a campaign all his loony concentration. It bothered him to leave his lookout, and he bounced from one foot to the other, deciding whether he would stay or go.

"C'mon," said Chop, and he gestured toward a pink and orange Dunkin' Donuts sign a quarter mile away, at the point where the Key West coastline bellied out and the dreary commercial strip began.

Squid calculated. It would take ten, twelve minutes to get there, score some coffee and a box of doughnuts, and get back to his post again. What were the odds? Not without ambivalence, he climbed into the Jag.

And while they were standing at the doughnut counter, discussing the merits of glazed and iced and Boston cream, Big Al Marracotta slipped unnoticed into town, his carsick rottweiler clawing at the windows of the Lincoln, his girlfriend refreshing her mascara, now that they had finally arrived.

Sunset approached.

Clouds flattened into slabs, spikes of sunlight slashed orange and rose and burgundy between them, a different color for each latitude of sky. Downtown the event was being celebrated as the climax of the day and the harbinger of cocktails, but for Alan Tuschman, still on the highway, heading west, it was mainly just a nuisance. Stoplights disappeared against the glare. Cruel rays shot through the smeared and eggy corpses of a million dead bugs on the windshield. His sunshade just missed being where the sun was, as sunshades always did, and he had to pee so badly that his solar plexus burned.

But at least he was very nearly at the Cow Key Bridge, the stubby gangplank to Key West.

On the far side of that bridge, Chop Parilla, bored into a trance, his Jag backed partway into mangroves, was looking toward the road, coveting selected vehicles, noting the tricks the red sun played on the pebbly reflective surfaces of the license plates.

Sid the Squid, jazzed up on caffeine, grease, and sugar, was pacing along the boundary where road shoulder softened into muck, sniffing low tide and the residue of hot tires while he scanned the stream of traffic.

Then, suddenly, at the moment when the sunshine went woolly in horizon haze, there it was: the long-awaited license plate, a hundred yards away, its shining letters filling up Sid's bulging eyes. BIG AL. NEW JERSEY. GARDEN STATE.

Berman's neck locked and his haunches quivered like a pointer's. He dove into the idling Jag just as the target car passed by. Chop Parilla peeled onto the highway, compressing him against his seat before his door was even closed.

"Hot shit," Chop said. "Lexuses I like. Best Jap car there is."

But tailing Alan Tuschman turned out to be too easy to be fun. He was tired and he didn't know where he was going. He crawled in the right lane the whole way down the Boulevard, his brake lights flashing now and then for no apparent reason.

At White Street, the boundary of Old Town, he pulled into a gas station, not up to the pumps, but to the curb next to the convenience store.

Thinking fast, Chop Parilla nosed the Jag next to the air hose. Squid Berman, on the pretext of checking the pressure in the tires, got out and crabbed along the warm and oily ground. He stayed there, low, kowtowing, as Alan Tuschman unfolded himself from his Lexus.

The tall man exited the car in stages. It took a long time. Big feet and fibrous ankles touched down on the pavement; a head of curly black hair dipped carefully beneath the door frame. Then he rose and the middle parts filled in: muttonlike thighs in snug black pants, a stretched thick torso that pulled at the buttons of a purple shirt. Rippling neck sinews festooned with gold; a strangler's veined and flexing hands, the furry fingers bearing rings.

Squid Berman, his eyeballs almost on the asphalt, looked steeply up and thought, Christ, he's huge.

Al Tuschman kicked one leg out, then the other. Hitched his pants up, sailor-style, with his forearms. The shih tzu jumped down from the car, sniffed around a moment, and squatted underneath a fender.

Squid Berman slipped back into the Jag as the furniture salesman, searching for a men's room, went into the convenience store. Chop Parilla said, "Fucker looks really tough. D'ya see the fuckin' wrists on the guy?"

Fear and excitement made moisture pool beneath Squid Berman's tongue. Damply he said, "Ya don't get the New York fish market lookin' like a wuss."

"Wuss?" Chop said, with a slightly nervous laugh. "Hey, I asked around about this guy, shit he did to convince Tony Eggs he's the guy to run the market."

"Like what?"

"Cut a deadbeat's nose off. Hand-fed it to his dog."

Squid stared at the shih tzu. It didn't seem the sort of creature that would eat pieces of a person's face, but with animals you never knew.

"'Nother guy," said Chop, "he had a problem using Tony Eggs' trucks. Big Al shipped 'im back from Montauk packed in ice between two tunas." He paused, had a sudden misgiving. "Mighta been swordfish. He catches us, we're fucked."

Squid hotly rubbed his hands together, yanked on each of his thumbs. "He ain't gonna catch us. I brought disguises."

Chop nodded absently, then turned his attention toward the Lexus. "Lives in Jersey. Figures. Needs a place to chill. Bet he has a huge house, big gate, doctors and dentists all around. What a fuckin' world, huh?"

A moment passed. Dusk was deepening, the lavender of sunset being elbowed aside by the orange of streetlamps. Squid stared off at the shih tzu, who was investigating shallow pools of transmission fluid, windshield detergent. Then he said, "Hey, wait a second. Didn't you tell me the guy was little and the dog was big?"

Parilla scratched his stomach. Detail was not his long suit except when it came to cars, and he didn't like admitting that maybe he was wrong. "Nah," he said, gesturing vaguely. "The dog is little. The guy is big."

Al Tuschman appeared once again in the doorway of the store. His shoulders blocked the light and he towered above a clerk who was gesturing directions.

Squid quibbled, "I coulda swore you said—"

Chop Parilla cut him off, slipping the Jag into gear as his quarry moved back toward the Lexus. "Squid, hey—can ya argue with a license plate?"

4

Big Al Marracotta, fortunate and lusty, had arrived in time to stash his queasy rottweiler in the Conch House kennel, to lose his Lincoln in the hotel's dark garage, then to enjoy the sunset from the rooftop bar, seven stories above the middle of Duval Street.

He and Katy sipped champagne and nibbled the obligatory fritters as a lounge pianist labored bravely, and the sun was doused in the pan-flat water out behind Tank Island. Al was happy. Key West. The air felt great and there were cocktail waitresses in fishnet hose, and some of them were female. New York was far enough away that he could forget about the headaches, the arguments, and remember only the good things. Rolling trucks. Tons of ice. Lobsters, crabs, and money. Seafood was a beautiful commodity. Delicious and perishable. Like life itself, but more so.

Al had timing. He was draining the last of the bubbly as the last of the red leached out of the clouds, leaving behind a blanket of slate gray. Without lowering his upturned flute, still hoping that a final drop might sizzle on his tongue, he said to his companion, "Nice, huh?"

"Very nice," said Katy. "Maybe we'll go out now, see the town?"

Al said, "First let's go downstairs awhile."

Katy dabbed her lips on a napkin to hide the pout.

They rose, and thereby became a spectacle. Katy had her high-heeled sandals on; they boosted her like afterburners. A high-tech bra made architecture of her bosom; Big Al could have worn her boobs as a cure for whiplash. Her waist came to his armpits, her spiky raven hair drew attention to his quarter inch salt-and-pepper helmet.

People watched as the two of them went by.

Big Al knew they did. Let 'em look, he figured. He liked it. Let 'em eat their hearts out.

Chop Parilla kept his gaze locked on Alan Tuschman's vanity plate as the short convoy continued down Truman Avenue.

At Elizabeth Street, the Lexus took a right and headed toward the Gulf. After eight or ten uncertain blocks, with a narrow slice of the waterfront coming into view, the salesman found, on the left side of the street, the sign that he'd been searching for. It was made of cypress wood, discreetly lit by soft floods bedded in shrubbery below. Immodestly, the sign proclaimed a single word: PARADISE.

Squid Berman could not let that slide. "His own little corner of hell is gonna be more like it," he said.

They watched Big Al pull into the parking area that was open to the street and paved in gravel. Then, unnoticed in the twilight, they slowly drove away.

Al Tuschman, weary from the road, switched off his ignition, picked up his suitcase and his dog, and trudged toward the office.

While he was filling out the registration card, the desk clerk asked him cheerfully, "And how did you find us, Mr. Tuschman?"

Without looking up, Al said, "I won you."

"Won us?"

The tall man glanced up now, smiled winningly. The imminent mention of sales made him act the salesman. "Contest where I work. Selling furniture. Dinettes."

"Ah," said the clerk, and he tried not to frown. He had a shaved head and a row of ruby studs along one eyebrow. He'd worked at Paradise for five years, and derived a large part of his self-image from his job. It was important to him that the place was classy, that its clientele were of a certain standing. Promotional junkets for salesmen in shiny shirts and pinky rings—that didn't sit so well with him. He changed the subject, gestured toward the shih tzu sniffing quietly around the small but airy office. "The dog's okay as long as he's leashed—"

"She. Fifi."

"—as long as she's leashed in public areas."

"No problem," said Al.

"Breakfast is from seven-thirty till eleven, and clothing is optional at poolside."

"Excuse me?"

"Mr. Tuschman," said the clerk, allowing himself a note of condescension. "We try to give our guests a totally natural and relaxing experience. There are no televisions and no phones. No entertainment other than the sun and the beauty of the gardens."

"Any single women?"

The row of rubies quivered on the desk clerk's eyebrow. "Our guests are very mixed," he said. "We're proud of that. We don't believe in segregation. God forbid a straight person should witness two men kissing, two women giving each other back rubs. Here at Paradise we don't think that way."

Al Tuschman pursed his lips and blinked, put the pen down softly on the registration card. "Bear with me," he said. "I'm a little tired. Are you telling me that I broke my ass from the Fourth right through Columbus Day, worked extra Saturdays plus Thursday evenings to win a free trip to a gay nudist colony?"

Contemptuous of categories, the desk clerk held his ground. "We get a lot of Europeans," he said. "Now and then celebrities who just want to be left alone. This place exists so that people can be happy. That's our only mission."

"Mission?"

"May I help you with your bag?"

Big Al Marracotta's suite was on the top guest floor. It had a king-sized bed with canopy, two bathrooms, a slice of harbor view, and a giant television set.

As soon as he and Katy had trundled down from the rooftop bar, Big Al called the desk to rent a VCR. He suggested to Katy that she might like to put an outfit on.

"Which one?" she asked.

Big Al put a finger on his chin and a twinkle in his eye. "The calico, I think. Maybe we'll go Western."

She went to the bathroom to change. Big Al went to the satchel of porno tapes he'd brought down from New York.

The bellman hooked up the VCR, and when he'd left, Katy reemerged. Her outfit was a thong and a tiny bra that looked like they'd been cut out of a tablecloth from a rib joint. A frilly garter cinched one thigh, and she wore a big felt hat like Dale Evans.

Big Al got naked and they watched the movie, which prominently featured a horse. Katy was impressed, maybe even aroused, but she wasn't having that good a time, and after a while even Big Al noticed.

"Whatsa matter?" he asked as the horse and the heroine were contemplating something hard to believe.

"Oh, I don't know," said Katy, pushing back the wide brim of her hat. She pushed it with her knuckles, and the chin strap moved against her jaw, and for a second she looked like a real cowgirl. "Vacation. Ya know. I thought we'd see the town."

This hinted at a basic philosophical difference. Some people thought vacation was about the place they went. Others viewed it as respite, pure and simple, from the place they'd left behind. "We'll get to that," he said. "We'll see the town."

"When?"

Al's eyes were on the screen. Either it was trick photography or he hoped to shake that woman's hand someday. "Little while later."

Katy had been seeing Al around eight months now. Their average date lasted three, four hours. Usually it was dinner and bed. Sometimes it was drinks in places where everyone knew Al, came over in waves to say hello, to hold impromptu meetings, sometimes argue. Once in a while they spent a whole night together; very rarely, when he could concoct a story to tell his wife, a weekend. This was the first time they were traveling together. "Al," she said, "I know you're like, high-spirited, but I never realized you're an out-and-out sex fiend."

Big Al took this as a compliment. It showed. "And not just sex!" he said. "Food. Excitement. Going fast. Gambling. It's got juice in it, baby, I'm there!"

From the TV came a chorus of whinnying and human moans.

"Later?" Katy said. "Later can we see the town?"

"Sure we can. 'Course. Crab claws, beach, a little jazz, anything ya like."

The girlfriend pursed her lips. She knew that was as well as she was going to do. First what he wanted. Later what she wanted. Maybe.

Big Al's eyes were on the screen. His tongue flicked out to lick his lips. He said, "Next year, maybe, I can get away, we'll go out West."

"Next year, Al?" said Katy. It seemed improbable to her.

Above the moaning and the horse sounds, Al said vaguely, "Arizona. Colorado. Looks nice, no?"

⌐

A bewildered Al Tuschman, already wondering how to tell
Moe Kleiman to fire his fancy new travel agent, followed the clerk
out of the office, through the deserted courtyard, and around the
pool, whose water glowed an unearthly blue from the soft lights
beneath the surface. A mild breeze moved the shrubbery, drew
forth dusty, scratching sounds and the melancholy smell of used-
up flowers. Fifi stopped to investigate, wiggled her nose at the
tang of iodine, the sharpness of salt. Her master barely noticed.
Uncharacteristically, his mind was still sniffing around something the clerk had said. That happiness was a mission.

This was not the kind of thing Alan Tuschman generally
thought about. At home, schmoozing, doing business, obeying
habits and following routines, who had time? But here, now, on
vacation and by himself, the notion somehow tweaked him.
Probably because he thought it was ridiculous. Missions were
about active things, challenges, dangers. Catching a pass in
heavy traffic on third-and-six—that was a mission. Making the
layup and drawing the foul when your team was down by three—
that was a mission. But happiness? That was . . . what? An accident? A by-product? A prize? No—prizes, he'd won plenty.
Prizes, trophies—cobwebs made bridges between the heads and
elbows of his trophies; trophies were a different thing from happiness. He gave an audible harrumph that made the desk clerk
turn around and look at him a second.

They continued down a path lined with philodendrons so enormous that a dog the size of Fifi could have hid beneath each leaf. At the end of the path was a whitewashed bungalow.

The clerk unlocked the door, turned on a dimmered light switch to reveal a tropically tasteful suite. Wicker this and rattan that and bamboo the other. Al the furniture maven knew it was cheap stuff, borax, from the Philippines, from Thailand, but in this room it worked. A huge ceiling fan turned lazily enough to slow the pulse. A cozy alcove held a fluffy sofa with rain-forest upholstery. There was an outdoor shower framed in thatch. On the bureau, a platter of ripe fruits. On the raw wood walls a passable print of greenish women with greenish breasts, and a couple of flower paintings, coyly lewd.

The desk clerk left, smugly declining to be tipped, and Al, exhausted, lay down on the bed, his heel against the mattress seam. He thought he'd rest awhile, then go out. Margaritaville. Sloppy Joe's. He'd never been to Key West before, but he'd heard about those places. Fabled joints where inhibitions melted down and fell away, and bad behavior was applauded. Where women sucked cigars and cakewalked in wet T-shirts. Rubbed strangers with their bare knees, showed off intimate tattoos. Bartenders poured liqueurs down chutes of ice, and mouths became acquainted as they shared the sticky stuff. Every day was Mardi Gras, and the neighbors back at home would never know.

Al Tuschman lay there, resting, thinking, imagining the noise and the crush and the smoke, and gradually he realized that he wasn't going out. Not tonight. Didn't have the strength, the will. Arriving someplace new, alone—it wasn't all that easy. Smiling, being friendly, looking for a pickup or only a smile in return—a lot of the time it just seemed like one more game to win, one more sales pitch to deliver.

He kicked off his shoes. The dog, understanding that he was now down for the count, jumped up and joined him on the bed. Happiness, Al Tuschman caught himself thinking once again. A mission? Well, maybe. Who knew?

He looked up at the ceiling fan. If he squinted very hard he could stop the motion of the blades. The effort made him deliciously sleepy, and he didn't fight it. A week in Key West, he thought. Contentment, relaxation, pleasure. He'd get with the program. Tomorrow, maybe. Tomorrow, in daylight. After a long and peaceful and refreshing sleep . . .

While he slept, sometime after midnight, Squid Berman and Chop Parilla wreaked havoc on the Lexus, whose lease had two years, three months still to go, and which assessed stiff penalties for excessive or abnormal wear.

The attack was Squid's idea, and bore the stamp of his malicious artistry.

It began with fifty pounds of calamari, purchased at deep discount because it was getting old and turning faintly blue. The calamari was packed in ten-pound plastic bags that had the sodden lumpiness of the internal organs of someone who was very, very ill. When the bags were opened, there issued forth an ocean smell that, at first whiff, was not unpleasant, but soon grew tinged with unwholesome odors of metal and ammonia.

With the seafood stashed in Chop Parilla's trunk, they drove back to Paradise, using the Jag to block the view of Alan Tuschman's car. The street was quiet but for the humming of the streetlamps, and it took Squid Berman about half a minute to pick the lock of the target vehicle. The alarm wailed for three seconds before Chop disarmed it, and, as usual, no one paid attention anyway. Then Squid slipped into the driver's seat and got down to business.

Most guys, of course, would simply have dumped the calamari in the car and bolted. This would have been adequate to achieve the minimum goal of stinking up the car. But such slipshod workmanship would have appalled Squid Berman. He was there to make a statement, feverish to create. His eyes were rolling and his knuckly hands were twitching as he opened the first sack of seafood.

He started with the passenger seat. Carefully, he laid out a squid, tentacles forward. Next to it he placed another, tentacles behind. The two squids interlocked like tiles, and their own slime grouted them nicely to the leather. He pressed down row on row of calamari, making an upholstery of seafood, a rank mosaic gleaming opalescent in the streetlight. When the passenger side was finished, he stood up to do the driver's seat. Calamari forward, calamari back. The gummy creatures seemed to wriggle like paisleys, and the morning sun would bake them on for good. Calamari on the seat back. Calamari on the headrest. Teach this scumbag to serve rotten seafood to his friends.

Sid Berman lavished so much time on his creation that even Chop was getting nervous. Two guys spreading calamari in someone else's car in the middle of the night; this would be a hard thing to explain. Although one bag of goods was still unopened, he said at last, "Enough already, Squid."

Squid was too intent to look up. With too much moisture underneath his tongue, he said, "I've got enough left to spell out 'Fuck You' on the dashboard."

"I think he'll read that on the seats," Parilla said. "Come on, we're outa here."

Berman hesitated, sighed. In this life nothing was ever quite perfect. Never enough time, enough resources. That's just how it was. Shaking his head, he dumped the last ten pounds of calamari on the gas pedal, the brake.

He rose and closed the door. He took a moment to admire his macabre and slithery work. The tubes of calamari looked somehow like ranks of condoms dancing samba.

Moving toward the Jag, he sniffed his hands and said to Chop, "D'ya bring the whaddyacallit, Wash'n Dri?"

"Ah, shit," Parilla said. "Forgot."

"Bummer," said Squid, and wiped his slimy fingers on his pants.

6

Big Al Marracotta, a little lost inside his one-size hotel bathrobe, rang down for extra salsa for his scrambled eggs.

It was pretty early for extra salsa, but he was eager to get that spice thing going, that burn. He slathered butter on his toast, slurped coffee, and watched Katy pout. Today she had a right to pout, he admitted to himself. He'd promised that they'd see the town last night, and then he'd fallen immovably asleep. Well, what the hell. It had been a long day. Lotta driving. Lotta drinking. Lotta sex. A man was entitled to get tired. He'd make it up to her today.

"Tell ya what," he said, his lips glistening with butter. "We'll finish breakfast, skip the A.M. workout, see the town. How's that? Pick up the dog, check out the beach, do a little shopping. Whaddya say?"

Katy picked at the edges of her mango muffin. "Fine," she blandly said. Mornings were not her best time. Her raven hair, brittle from the dyeing, stood up here and there in random curlicues. With only smears of faded makeup, her eyes looked rather small and waifish. Her breasts felt heavy in the morning; they pulled down on her collarbones and reminded her that she was twenty-nine, and being kept in only so-so fashion by a terminally married man who, no doubt, would dump her fairly soon, by which time she'd be thirty, thirty-one, and what then?

Maybe Big Al was reading her mind. Maybe just trying to regain lost ground. He reached out gently and held her chin. His hand was small and surprisingly soft, the heel of it like a pillow. His touch could on occasion be infuriatingly tender. He said, "Come on. You're beautiful. Ya know that?"

She blinked. She could have cried. Instead she tried to smile, and when that didn't quite work out, she made a playful and ferocious face and bit his hand, the pillowy part between the wrist and thumb. Selfish bastard. Selfish bastard who could also sometimes be a charming bastard.

Big Al squirmed and pretended to wince as she nibbled on his hand, her small teeth leaving shallow dents in his flesh. It almost hurt; it did hurt, in a way that got him going, and he began to calculate just how much hell there'd be to pay if he took back his offer to skip the A.M. workout.

Alan Tuschman also woke up early.

He'd managed to slip beneath his light blanket, though not to get out of last night's clothes. Now he smelled damp earth and chlorine, and gradually remembered where he was. He opened his eyes to see his slowly turning ceiling fan, palm shadows flickering against his raw wood walls, greenish women with greenish breasts staring down at him with no great curiosity.

He stretched, his long hands and feet overreaching the confines of the bed. The dog licked his face. She wanted walking. He got up, washed, and went outside.

From behind its thatch enclosure, the pool pump softly hummed. Otherwise the courtyard of Paradise was quiet. Dew was shrinking back on enormous leaves as the sun climbed higher in the sky. A large woman sat lotus-style on a towel near the hot tub. Her eyes were closed and she didn't have a shirt on. She inhaled deeply and raised her arms, displaying furry armpits.

Across the way, the breakfast buffet was just being set up. Al caught a whiff of coffee and realized he was famished. He went over to investigate. There were thimble muffins and miniature croissants curled up like unripe fetuses and dainty little ramekins of fruit cup. It was all very cute but it didn't look like breakfast. Not to Al, who was used to Jersey diners. Danish big as hubcaps. Omelets the size of shoes. Home fries bleeding paprika, piled to the very edges of the plate.

He decided to go out to eat. He went back to his bungalow to grab his car keys. Then, with Fifi in the lead, he rounded the pool, trod the gravel path, and exited the gate to the parking area.

He took no special notice of the old hippie nodding out behind a buttonwood hedge across the street—the red bandanna wrapped around the long and stringy hair, the small, round Trotsky glasses worn far down on the nose. It was Sid the Squid, of course. He hadn't been able to sleep. Too excited. Hungry, like every artist, for a reaction to his efforts.

So he'd left Chop snoring in the mildewed motel room that they shared, and strolled to Paradise at dawn. Now he struggled not to fidget as Big Al approached the violated, sunstruck Lexus. Moisture pooled beneath Sid's tongue; he swallowed and his Adam's apple shuttled up and down.

Al Tuschman, tunelessly whistling, used his remote to unlock the driver's-side door. He'd reached out for the handle before he realized anything was wrong. Then he froze and squinted, disbelieving, through the windshield.

Sunshine was skidding across the sweep of glass, making it half mirror. Sky was reflected, and the restless crowns of palms; but light also penetrated, and what Al Tuschman saw behind the glare mocked all understanding. Calamari. Stale, dry calamari, spoiled to a sickly mottled gray, glued in wavy patterns to the leased leather of his seats. Scallops of scum marked the places where dead tentacles had shrunk back in the tropic heat. The black dots of eyestalks stood out creepily against the tasteful taupe.

Across the street, Squid Berman squirmed and swallowed, trying not to wet his pants or let out a whoop of glee.

Al Tuschman opened the car door. Fifi, by long habit, jumped up toward the seat, then seemed somehow to reverse field, midair, and pulled away, whimpering, to the limit of her leash. She'd smelled a stink that seemed to be the vapor of death itself. Ocean turned to ammoniac poison. Nourishment corrupted to putrescent goo.

Al Tuschman sucked in a tiny sniff that brought tears to his eyes. He stopped breathing. Yet some compulsion, some need for confirmation, led him to reach out a thick finger to touch the calamari. The tubes felt stiff and starchy, like undercooked lasagna. The tentacles were dank and crusty and bore a disgusting resemblance to something secretly discovered in one's nose.

Al closed the door, wiped his eyes, turned in a different direction to inhale.

Across the street, Squid Berman rejoiced and waited for the inevitable explosion, the operatic tantrum. In his world, men had magnificent and primal tempers that gave rise to absurd and highly entertaining displays. When something bad happened to them, they screamed, cursed, turned red, kicked walls, punched doors, swore revenge, and railed at heaven. It was great to watch.

But Al Tuschman did none of these things.

He didn't have much of a temper. Not anymore, having spent so much adrenaline on the ballfields of his youth. Besides, innocent, clear of conscience, he had no reason to suspect malice. So he wasn't thinking about revenge; as his mind gradually cleared, he began instead to think about insurance. What was the deductible on calamari? What if he needed a whole new interior? He rubbed his chin, wondered how he'd schmooze the lease people on this one. He shuffled his feet in the gravel. As if it mattered, he pulled out the remote and locked the car again.

Squid Berman watched him from behind the buttonwood, and his disappointment at the absence of a show turned moment by moment to grudging admiration. He thought: Christ, this guy is really cool. Calculating; patient. Made sense. Tough and cool—that was the combination that brought guys to the top. The hotheads, they went just so far before burning out or making a fatal blunder. . . . Besides, this guy was probably so fucking rich— what was a brand-new Lexus to him?

Squid retreated behind the hedge, choked back a private embarrassment that his initial ploy had fallen short, that his masterpiece of seafood had elicited barely a grumble from his prey. He was let down but not discouraged. He liked a challenge. Big Al was cool and rich, unflappable? Fine. Sid Berman would find a way to get to him. No problem. He'd just have to get some rest and try a little harder.

7

There were times when shopping was about acquiring needed things, and times when it was a desperate search for comforts true or false, and times when it was first and foremost an exercise in spite. The expedition that carried Katy Sansone up and down Duval Street, Big Al and Ripper at her side, was of this final type.

She wasn't getting what she wanted from this trip. Not at all. She hadn't been on the beach yet, even for a second. She hadn't seen the ocean except for slices of it from the cocktail lounge or through the window of her room as she lay there on her back. It was his trip, his vacation.

Well, what had she expected? The question mocked her, but she couldn't let it go. How had she imagined it would be? What did she think or hope she might get out of it? The awful truth was that, if she was going to cut through the fibs and poses and excuses and just be deadly honest, what she'd really wanted from this trip was not about beach and not about ocean and not about a suntan.

It was about romance.

There, she'd admitted it. Romance. It was ridiculous, pathetic, and she knew it was pathetic. Of course she did. She'd wanted to feel special. Ha. With Big Al? Whose idea of romance, maybe, was to light a candle before he poked her. Clink champagne glasses before the porno films came out. Before he washed

himself and combed his hair and went back to his fat wife in Bay
Ridge. This was romance? This was what people wrote songs
about? Katy wished she was either a little smarter or a whole lot
dumber. Little smarter, maybe she wouldn't have got herself into
such a jerky situation. Dumber, maybe it wouldn't gnaw at her
so much. As it was . . .

As it was, she promenaded up and down Duval Street, shopping with grim and joyless fury. Designer sunglasses that made
her look either like a European actress or a total geek. Wrap-
around skirts whose ease of removal caused Big Al to lick his
sloppy lips. A dolphin brooch; fake Spanish coins set into ear-
rings. With each purchase, she looked sideways at her sugar
daddy, trying to determine if she'd succeeded yet in annoying
him, had managed to spend enough of his money so that he
would reveal discomfort, and she could feel that she was somehow winning.

The strategy failed utterly, as she secretly knew it would. Big
Al, swaggering along, flanked by his big-balled rottweiler and his
tall young squeeze, got only happier and more puffed up as they
shopped. Buying power was a beautiful thing. A potent thing.
There was sex in a wad of fifties. Throwing dough at his girlfriend's whims didn't bother him at all. It tightened his grip and
therefore made him frisky.

At some point, with shopping bags chafing against her thin
and still-pale legs, Katy understood she was just digging herself
in deeper. She got depressed. The sun was high, the fresh part of
the morning had been wasted, and what had she accomplished?
Got some things that, after Al got bored and dumped her, she'd
never want to see again anyway. "I'm ready to go back," she said.

Big Al, on a spending roll, was surprised. "Already?" he said.
"There's nothing else ya want?"

"Nothing I'm gonna find here," said Katy.

Big Al blinked up at her, and for some part of a second she
thought perhaps he'd understood. Then he said, "Where, then?
Miami?"

"Al," she said, "I'd like to get out of these shoes."

That, he understood. He shrugged and they headed back toward the Conch House, Ripper's testicles bouncing proudly as they went.

Alan Tuschman, disgusted, baffled, trudged into the office of Paradise and asked the clerk to call the cops.

The clerk seemed unsurprised and maybe even pleased that the slightly thuggish-looking salesman was having trouble. Unctuously, he said, "Is something wrong?"

"Nah," said Al, "just thought I'd say hello."

This was exactly the sort of Northeast sarcasm the clerk had moved down from suburban Philadelphia to avoid. He averted his gaze and made the call. Al went back outside and leaned against the trunk of his despoiled car. The old hippie across the way was gone.

A motorcycle cop roared up in about ten minutes. The short-legged officer climbed off the bike like a pug addressing a fire hydrant. He looked at Al accusingly. "What's the problem?"

Al pointed through the driver's-side window of the Lexus.

The cop clomped over in his boots and squinted through his Ray-Bans. "What is it?"

"Calamari. Wanna smell?"

The cop said no.

"Crazy, huh?" said Al.

The cop didn't offer an opinion.

"Something like this," Al asked, "why would it happen?"

The cop scratched his head right through the helmet. Then he began an expert examination of the car. He determined that it was new and pricey and from a Northern state held in universal and profound contempt. "Town like this," he said, "there's a certain amount of vandalism against tourists. Resentment, ya know. Hate."

Al Tuschman gave a worldly nod. To be resented, detested,

mocked, and victimized—why else did anybody take vacation? He said, "Any chance of fingerprints?"

Sharply, the cop said, "D'ya touch the door handle?"

He had Al there. He pressed the attack.

"Anybody mad at ya?"

"I just got here."

"Hot climate," said the cop, "it don't take long for people to get mad. Ya look too long at someone's girlfriend's titties? Get talkin' politics with shrimpers?"

Al had not yet had food or coffee. He was hatching a headache and he wished he was home. He said, "Look, if I could just get a report. For insurance."

The cop produced a pad, began scrawling. Now he pretended to be helpful. "I was you, I'd call a dealer."

"Got one here in town?"

"Fancy car like this, closest one's Miami. Sun, I think it's called." He paused, and Al Tuschman tried to believe he didn't see a quick malevolent flash behind the Ray-Bans. "Towing cost ya six, eight hundred bucks."

The cop snapped the report from his pad and roared off on his motorbike.

Al Tuschman stuffed the paper into his pocket, went back into the office, called the dealer in Miami. The towing, as it turned out, would cost a mere five hundred seventeen bucks. Al left the car key with the desk clerk.

"Who should I give it to?" the man with the shaved head asked.

"Anyone that wants it," said Al disgustedly.

The clerk bit his lip. What a sarcastic guy, he thought, as his big, rough-looking guest pivoted on aching knees and left.

Back in his mildewed motel room, Chop Parilla was more than half asleep. A sweaty sheet clung to his hairy back; its wrinkles seemed to continue in the thick skin of his stub of neck. Fugitive shafts of light and the dull hum of traffic from the Boulevard were prying him out of the millionth version of his favorite dream—a dream of weightless sex amid the knobs and gauges of a stolen car, never the same car twice.

In his mind he copped a final feel of the dashboard and kissed the dream good-bye. Then he heard the doorknob rattle and he reached by reflex for the revolver underneath his pillow.

As the door swung open and a rude wedge of sunshine cut into the room, he came up on an elbow, cocked the hammer of the gun, and drew a bead on a greasy-haired hippie with a red bandanna and stupid-looking little glasses way down on his nose.

"Hey, don't fuck around. It's me."

Squid Berman was slurping coffee from one of a pair of Styrofoam cups. He handed the other to Chop, who put the gun down on the nightstand. Squid tore off the bandanna and the wig, polished off his java, and started pacing the narrow alley between the single beds.

"So how'd it go?" Parilla asked.

"Went shitty," Squid admitted. "Went weird. The fucker hardly flinched!"

Chop rubbed the pads of fat beneath his eyes. "I'm not surprised."

"Whaddya mean, you're not surprised? Bullshit you're not surprised."

Calmly, Chop said, "Ya don't get the fish market goin' off half-cocked."

Squid paced faster, pivoted more furiously. "He acted like it was, I don't know, a mosquito bite. Closes the car door. Doesn't even slam it. Rubs his chin. Fuckin' philosophical."

"Smart," said Chop. "Ya don't just get mad. Ya give it time. Ya get *really* mad. Ya find out who to hurt. Then ya let it out. That's the smart way to get mad."

"Watches the dog take a leak," said Squid. "Strolls back to the hotel. Like ho-hum, just another fuckin' morning . . . A gorgeous piece a work like what I did, and the fucker barely flinches!"

Chop sipped coffee, rearranged the damp sheet that lay across his butt. "Ya want I should call Nicky, ask advice?"

"Don't insult me, Chop."

"Hey, it's just that Nicky knows 'im better."

"Not half as good as I'm gonna know 'im by the time I'm through. I'm goin' to school on the sonofabitch. I'm learnin' every minute."

"And what ya learned so far?" Chop challenged.

"Possessions, which is money, he don't care about," said Squid. "So what's that leave? His dignity. His person. I'll find a way in, Chop. I'll make 'im nuts."

"Enough with the pacing, Squid. You're makin' me a little nuts."

The bandy man kept doing laps. "You'll see. You'll see. Have I ever let ya down before?"

Q

Al Tuschman surprised himself by not being more upset. Maybe it was just that food and coffee sufficed to make a hungry person happy, brought life back to basics.

He'd found a good breakfast place down on Duval Street. A courtyard a few steps up from the sidewalk. Outdoors, he could sit with Fifi, and, even better, the place had the kind of stuff that he was used to. God bless the Greeks. They had one recipe for home fries, disseminated it around the globe. Used the same take-out cups in Florida as in Jersey: blue background with a white acropolis, the seam of the cup always slicing through a statue's crotch.

Comforted by these familiar things, Al felt himself becoming more receptive to the newness parading before him.

Drag queens who hadn't been to sleep yet. Homeless guys tying up their mildewed bedrolls. Miserable youths with baggy pants, rings through their noses and tattoos on their feet. And the inevitable mismatched couples. Slight men with wide women. Brassy women with mousy men. Here a tall and chesty babe weighed down with shopping bags, on the arm of a grinning short guy who might have been her uncle, leading a rottweiler whose fleeting nearness made Fifi tick her paws against the gravel of the courtyard. The woman met his eye, held it for some fraction of a second. He thought he saw a quick twitch at the corner of her mouth. But she didn't seem to be flirting; more like apologizing for something.

A funny town, Al decided. He went back to his eggs and tried not to think about his car. Or, if he had to think about it, to find a way to rationalize what the towing and the deductible would cost him. Less than a Florida vacation. So he was still ahead. Sort of. Then again, he wouldn't be on vacation, certainly not on this vacation, if he'd had to pay for it.

Was that good or bad, he wondered—that he wouldn't take vacation unless he won it? Did it mean he was a workaholic, or just cheap? Was it that he didn't have a lady to take vacation with? Or was he simply the kind of guy who didn't like vacations? And why did that seem somehow shameful to admit?

He finished his omelet, paid his tab, and rose to leave.

But that was another thing about being on vacation—now that breakfast was over, he had no idea what his next activity should be, or what it would accomplish.

For a moment, he stood there indecisive, slowly wobbling like a bothered compass. Finally an ancient instinct steered him toward the water and he joined the stream that brainlessly headed down Duval, vaguely aware that in so doing, he had become a part of the tourist show, a big, burly, lonely guy, still in Northern pants, his only friend a fussy and unlikely little dog.

"The beach?" Big Al Marracotta had said dismissively. "Who needs it? Sand in your crack? Riffraff all around. No place to get a cocktail . . . Come on. Right here we got the pool, the swim-up bar. Beautiful."

Katy Sansone had pouted but decided not to argue. If she was ever going to have her way about anything, she had to pick her battles. Besides, could she explain to him how she felt about the difference between the ocean and the pool? Something vast and alive as opposed to something filtered and contained? Something full of mystery and romance compared with something tourists' children peed in? A blue and infinite horizon instead of a view of the lanai rooms behind the towel kiosk and the row of lounge chairs? She felt those things but she knew she wouldn't explain them very well, and Big Al would look at her like she was crazy.

So she'd sighed, pulled on her thong, settled it between her buttocks, slipped into a shift, and gone down to the pool.

Big Al at least was happy there, as usual.

He had a boxer-style bathing suit with a mesh cup that left him room to breathe. A Knicks cap kept the sun out of his eyes. He could look at the water cascading down women's cleavages as they pulled themselves out of the pool. Katy let him rest his knuckles against her bare hip, as long as he was careful not to leave some bizarre handprint of a tan line on her butt.

Sunshine and near-nudity. For Big Al this was heaven. He lay back on his lounge till he was good and sweaty, then waded, thigh-deep, into the pool. Tepid water. Beautiful. The sun had made him thirsty. "Cocktail?"

Katy squinted toward him. She doubted it was noon and she didn't want a drink. Problem was, it was hard to say no without a reason, and reasons to say no got only harder to find.

She joined him in the pool. They waded to the bar. Water reached her navel and Big Al Marracotta's nipples. He ordered piña coladas.

When the drinks were made, he squinted down, pushed aside the paper umbrella, and sucked his cocktail through a straw. Then, almost boyishly, he smiled at the sweetness of it, the cloy of coconut, the slushiness of pineapple. Smiled as though he had a virgin conscience and not a problem in the world.

In fact he had at least one quite serious problem; he just didn't know it yet.

His problem was that, at that very moment, Benny Franco, the guy he'd left in charge of the fish market in his absence, was having his rights read to him as he was bundled into a government Plymouth and carted off to the Metropolitan Correction Center.

In New York, Benny's arrest was regarded as a slight surprise. There'd been rumors, speculation. The feds had been looking pretty closely at his pre-seafood careers in paving and trash carting. Had noted certain patterns—a consistent lack of gusto in the bidding process if Benny was involved; a tendency of determined competitors to undergo misfortune. These patterns did not place Benny in a flattering light.

But no one had expected the indictment to come down quite so soon; and even though Benny Franco would be out on bail before the sun went down, his arrest was a nuisance. It didn't do to have a guy who'd just been indicted on racketeering charges running, even temporarily, such a visible enterprise as the wholesale fish market. The connection might lead people wrongly to imagine that their seafood was tainted by the raunchy hands of organized crime.

This, at least, was the position taken by Carlo Ganucci, the gaunt and ancient *consigliere* of the Calabrese family. "Don't look right," he said to Tony Eggs Salento, the *capo di tutti capi,* as they sat on folding chairs in the back room of their social club on Prince Street. "Guy's name gets inna paper. Place of employment: Fulton Fish. People like put two and two together."

"Fuck is Big Al at?" Tony Eggs demanded. He was an old-style boss, though he'd risen to the top only recently, as the flashy, newer-style bosses became celebrities and, one by one, were put away forever. Tony Eggs knew enough to stay in the background. He didn't go to nightclubs and wasn't photogenic. He wore undistinguished suits and plain white shirts and let hair grow out of his ears and nose. He was so somber and so glum that nobody was jealous of his power. He was known for being starkly fair and unforgiving, and he had a work ethic like the guy who beat the drum in Roman galleys.

"Flahda," said the *consigliere.* The skin on his face was pale and paper-thin. You could see his skull move when he talked. "Took vacation."

"Vacation," said Tony Eggs with contempt. To him there was a dark satisfaction and a grim responsibility in a mobster's work. Since when did mobsters take vacation?

"Ya want we call 'im home? Might take a day or two to find 'im."

Tony Eggs pulled on his face. It was a long and fleshy face and it stretched considerably as he pulled it. "Who else we got could run the show awhile?"

Ganucci thought it over. Not that there were many people to choose from; not anymore. But it could be a headache if they put in the wrong guy, someone who was not respected.

The boss tugged his chin, fretted with the short black hairs protruding from his nostrils, and answered his own question. "There's Nicky."

"That's true," Ganucci said. "'Course, ya fired him before."

"Never said he wasn't good at what he did."

There was a pause, then the *consigliere* said, "Well, ya don't mind my sayin' so, I never quite understood why ya took it away from him then."

Tony Eggs leaned far back in his chair, interwove his fingers, stretched them inside out so that the knuckles cracked. "He liked it too much. *Capice?*"

Ganucci wasn't sure he did.

"He bragged about it," the boss went on. "Strutted. Gettin' in his mind like a fuckin' movie star. When I heard he's goin' ta Gotti's tailor, I said, *basta,* that's it."

Traffic noise filtered in from the street. In the front room of the club someone was shuffling cards.

The *consigliere* cleared his throat. "Tony," he said. "Nicky liked the job too much before. It worry you at all that maybe he'll remember just how much he liked it?"

The boss pulled on an earlobe.

"Ya know," the ancient counselor went on. "Like maybe make a problem between him and Al?"

Tony shrugged. In the shrug was the patient, durable malice that comes with disapproval. "No one put a gun to Big Al's head," he said, "and tol' 'im that he hadda take vacation."

9

Al Tuschman finally got into bathing trunks and sat out by the pool at Paradise. Sitting there, his dog splayed out in the shade beneath his lounge, he felt torn between looking at everything and looking at absolutely nothing.

He could not help noticing that everyone but him was rubbing someone else. Over by the deep end of the pool, two men were taking turns rubbing sunscreen on each other's shoulders; Al scared himself by acknowledging a certain elegance in their gleaming skins and leanly muscled arms. Nearer the hot tub, a topless woman was doing something mysterious and sensual to another woman's feet; he could faintly hear the rubbed woman occasionally chanting.

Then there was the naked threesome. Two women, one guy. Breasts everywhere; a tanned, confusing minefield of breasts. The threesome had towels draped carelessly about their loins, but face it, they were naked. They spoke a foreign language, which heightened Al Tuschman's feeling that he had somehow stumbled into one of those slow and moody European films that he never understood. Decadence: Good or bad? Seemed pretty pleasant—so why did someone always blow his brains out at the end? The threesome talked softly but with animation. They giggled a lot. Were they witty or slaphappy? Sophisticated or just plain crazy? And was Al a bourgeois prude, or was what he was feeling a thin mask for envy, pure and simple?

There was neither profit nor resolution to these thoughts, but at least they kept Al occupied while Chop Parilla, not fifty yards away on the far side of a frail reed fence, was hijacking the tow truck that had come to fetch his car.

It was an impulsive maneuver, totally unplanned.

Chop and Squid had been staked out in the shade, sitting in the Jag. Squid wore a paper hat and a white apron that looped around his neck and tied at the waist; it was the look he needed for his next assault on Big Al's sanity. While they were waiting for an opportunity to put this next phase into effect, the flatbed from Sun Motors in Miami pulled up.

The driver—lanky, sweating, and with a shirttail out—parked next to the ravaged Lexus, then went into the hotel office.

Chop eyed the spotless stamped aluminum of the flatbed. Then he turned to Squid, his face flushed and his voice breathy. "If he's here for the Lex, I'm stealin' it."

Squid frowned so vigorously that the paper hat shifted behind his pointy ears. "Stealin' cars," he said, "that ain't the job."

"Look the opportunity," Chop argued.

Squid maintained a solid silence.

"It ain't *botherin'* the job," Chop pleaded. "Take two minutes."

Squid swallowed; his Adam's apple shuttled up and down. He said, "How long it takes, that ain't the point. It's fuckin' with my concentration. Ya wanna do somethin' right, ya do one thing at a time."

Chop drummed on the steering wheel and sucked his teeth as he watched the driver come back from the office, a key now dangling from his hand. The driver opened the Lexus' door, quickly stepped back at the stench. He shook his head and reached in just long enough to put the car in neutral, then climbed into his truck and maneuvered it into a position from which he could winch the pillaged vehicle onto the flatbed.

Parilla was stewing. Whose gig was this anyway, and why was he suddenly taking orders from Squid? He squirmed as the greased piston lifted and the flatbed tilted down; he plucked the damp shirt from his armpits as the driver came around from the cab and grabbed the towing cables with their awesome hooks. Finally he said, "Wit' all due respect to your fuckin' concentration, fuck you, it's meant to be, I'm goin' for it."

Squid just rolled his bulging eyes. Chop reached across and moved his gun from the glove box to the waistband of his pants.

He waited until the driver had laid down on the gravel to attach the cables to the Lexus, until he was helpless and in shadow.

Then he sprang from the Jag, walking quickly but not running. He dropped to his knees next to the prone driver, down at the level of axle grease and undercoating and the smell of tires. He hid his revolver with his body as he freed it from his pants, and stuck the muzzle of it in the driver's ear.

Softly he said, "Don't make a sound and don't move a muscle."

The driver flinched, then went rigid as a fish beached in sunshine.

"This is my car you're fuckin' with," Chop whispered.

"You make mistake, I think," the driver managed. "I have order to pick up this car."

Chop pushed the gun a little harder. "You don't understand. All cars are my cars. What's your name?"

"Ernesto."

"You a Teamster, Ernesto?"

"Sí."

"Good. I get along with Teamsters." He put some fresh pressure on the muzzle and dug a knee into the small of the prone man's back. "This can be easy or this can be hard, Ernesto. How would you like it to be?"

The driver didn't have much breath left. "Eassy," he wheezed.

"Good man. Tell ya what. I'm gonna give you three hundred dollars and hurt you just enough to make you a fuckin' hero. That okay with you, Ernesto?"

"Hokay."

"Now be a pro. Jack the fuckin' car up and let's get onna road."

Squid Berman watched them pull away. Chop was good, he had to admit it. The gun never showed. Anybody passing would have figured he was down there helping. The whole move was crisp, efficient, practiced. Now Chop would call his boys in Hialeah for a pickup. The flatbed would drive down some deserted road. Chop would give the driver his cash, a black eye, and a shallow slice that would hardly need stitches. Neat.

Neat but conventional, thought Squid, pulling on his knuckles, straightening his apron. A formula. The work of a craftsman, not an artist. He resettled his paper hat behind his ears and refocused his attention on the entrance of Paradise.

What he himself was doing with this caper was on a whole different level, of course. The level of real invention, true improvisation. It was jazz to other guys' whistling. Did Chop realize that? he wondered. Did anybody?

By the time the afternoon shadows overtook the Conch House pool, Big Al Marracotta had had four piña coladas, and was in the grip of a salacious mix of wooziness and lust. His shoulders were sunburned, and he liked the heat. The cup of his bathing suit was damp, and he liked the cool. He liked the thighs of other men's wives and girlfriends as they scissored and lifted on their lounges, he liked the bare nearness of Katy's pinkened behind, and he was ready to go upstairs awhile.

Up in their suite, before he'd even got out of his wet trunks, he went straight to his satchel of tapes. He riffled through the black plastic boxes, lips pursed as he considered. Discipline? Chinese? Finally he said to Katy, "Feel a little . . . futuristic?"

She looked at him a moment before she answered. Drained and mellowed by the sun, she made an effort to think kindly of him, and gently of herself for falling in with him. She tried to remember his good points. That twinkle in the eye. A certain generosity that every now and then seemed separate from strutting or control. An unflagging and unthinking zest that amused her and that she envied. Who wouldn't? She managed a somewhat weary smile and went off to the bathroom.

She returned looking like a sunburned outtake from *Barbarella.* Reinforced conic bra in space-age silver. Strapped and shiny panties that suggested something gladiatorial. Arm-cinching bracelets from which dangled disks resembling electrodes.

"You are something else," Big Al said, flicking his tongue between the gap in his front teeth.

The movie was called *Sex Trek.* Its premise was that the future would be a very phallic era, and that technological advances would largely focus on bold new designs in marital aids.

Leaning back on stacked-up pillows, his hand on Katy's thigh and his eyes glued to the screen, Big Al Marracotta said, "Jesus, will ya look at that? Solar-powered. Gets 'er everywhere at once!"

Katy looked from the TV to the stymied golden light captured in the curtained window, and wondered if they'd finish up in time to see the sunset.

10

Dusk. Al Tuschman stood in the outdoor shower, which was framed in thatch and ended at his knees. He soaped his armpits, watched sudsy water slide off the slatted boards beneath his feet. The light was soft and violet; the air was the same temperature as his skin and smelled of fruits and flowers.

Al shampooed his coarse, curly hair and finally let his mind acknowledge what his body already knew: Key West was getting to him. All that bare skin. All that rubbing. All those pretty sunburned necks and unfettered pendant breasts with tan lines halfway down them. The lack of hurry. The lack of purpose, except for the staunchly unembarrassed purpose of feeling good. Happiness as mission. All this had been sexing him up from the moment he arrived.

Now he no longer had excuses for failing to get out there and do something about it. He had his bearings. He was rested. This was the evening he would do the bars and try to meet a woman.

He rinsed, turned off the shower, and stepped into the bathroom, where he dried himself and shaved. Shaving, he appraised his face. The pits and bumps of adolescent acne; the scattered crescent scars of energetic youth. The very first gray hairs just now sprouting at the temples. A face that had seen some life, that had some life to offer in return. It worked for him on the sales floor.

But in bars? In bars the salesman tended to get shy. Flinched sometimes at soulful stares. Needed help to jump-start conversations. Sometimes drank too much to loosen up, then got morose instead of suave. Or, very occasionally, suave till he couldn't stand himself. Still, a person had to try. . . .

He dressed. Pulled on snug pants that showed the contours of his athlete's legs while revealing nothing of the aches and creaks. A tight blue shirt, the creases where it had been folded soon stretched and steamed away by the bulk of his chest. Chain; rings; loafers. A last tousle of his hair, and he was ready. He put Fifi's leash on, waved to annoy the dozing desk clerk as he passed the office, and headed out to start the evening with some solid food.

Squid Berman, still, with obsessive patience, waiting in the Jag, watched him head off down Elizabeth Street, teased himself with the danger implicit in the tough guy's wide shoulders and his rolling gait. He sat tight until he saw Big Al round the corner.

Then, opening a cooler in the backseat, he grabbed a shopping bag, smoothed his apron and straightened out his paper hat, and walked through the gate of Paradise as if he owned the place.

He went into the office and told the clerk he had a delivery for the gentleman who just went out.

The clerk blinked himself out of his catnap, studs quivering on his eyebrow. "I'll hold it for him here."

"He asked me special to leave it by his door," said Squid.

"That really isn't necessary."

"It is."

"Is what?"

"Necessary."

There was a momentary standoff.

"What I'm delivering," Squid resumed, "it needs, very important, it needs, uh, moonlight."

"Moonlight?"

"Orchid. Very rare. Expensive. Real expensive. Needs moon-

light or it dies. In minutes. Said I should leave it in the moonlight by his door."

The clerk furrowed his brow. The wrinkles went all up his
shaved head.

"So please," Squid said, "point me to the room. You wanna be
responsible it dies? Come on, it's too long in the bag already."

The clerk frowned at the bag, which, oddly, made a sudden
paper sound, a scratch. He wondered why it was always the least
classy guests who made the most trouble, then sighed and did as
he was asked.

Squid skirted the blue pool, went down the path that led to
Big Al's bungalow. Hidden by foliage, he slipped around to the
side, crawled under the thatch of the outdoor shower, scrabbled
along the still-damp slatted boards. He prepared to shoulder in
the bathroom door, but Big Al hadn't bothered to lock it.

The gremlin sniffed at his quarry's aftershave, worked a splinter into his bar of soap, then slipped into the bedroom and made
himself at home.

Al started with a beer or two, tried a frozen margarita, then
switched over to Sambuca. But it was one of those nights when
he couldn't get comfortable with a drink, and he couldn't get
comfortable with a place.

It wasn't even eleven yet, and he was already in his third
joint. The first had been cheesily festive and way too loud, with
amplifiers hanging from the ceiling, sound waves seeming to
blow the smoke around. The second featured the music of his
youth, which didn't make him feel young or nostalgic, but rather
anxious and sad and weighed down with a secret. Made him
think about football games, the shameful thing that no one ever
knew. He was scared. Scared every time the ball was thrown to
him. The pressure not to blow the catch. The inevitable impact,
the skidding, scraping collision with the cold, damp ground.
Same with crashing the boards in basketball season. Smashed

fingers; elbows in his nose and eyes. Scared every time. Big tough guy. Schoolboy hero . . . A softie. He didn't need to hear seventies music ever again.

This third place suited him better. It was dim and moody. Grown-up. It didn't pretend to be a party. Jazz was playing, and jazz was different every time, it didn't freeze you in a moment like pop songs, which never changed, which were stuck in their old neighborhood forever. He started to relax.

Relaxing, he felt sexy again. Feeling sexy, he was frustrated. Frustrated, he kept drinking. Drinking, he wavered between gloom, excessive confidence, and an increased capacity to be smooth, silly, or both together.

That's when the two women came in and sat down near him. They were no younger than himself, possibly a few years older. He smiled at them as they sat and they sort of smiled back, then pulled their eyes away. They ordered vodkas, lit up cigarettes, and started talking.

By their second round they were talking louder and Al was leaning subtly toward them.

"Don't get me wrong," one of them was saying. She had wonderful thick hair that rose up in a single wave, dark brown with unapologetic flecks of gray. "I don't hate men. I like men. In fact, I prefer men, all in all. It's just that men are kinky."

The other woman rattled her ice cubes. She had a tan and bony face closely framed in lank pale hair. Al didn't like her nostrils, which were flat as the nose holes of a skeleton. "You can't just generalize like that," she said.

"Oh yes I can," the other woman answered and lit another cigarette. She squinted at the smoke, which made Al realize how big and round her eyes had been when they were fully opened. "Look, I know the pattern," she went on. "At first it's lovey-dovey, aiming at the conquest of the body. You know, straight from high school. Getting in. But then right away it's head games, toys—".

"Hey," the lank-haired woman interrupted with a soft but bawdy giggle, "women too, there's a lot of . . . let's say improvising."

Al Tuschman sipped his 'Buca. He was dying.

"That's different," argued the woman with the wonderful thick hair.

"What's different?" said the woman with the nose holes, gesturing for more drinks. "The body's the body and the mind's the mind."

The thick-haired woman was groping for an explanation. She ran a hand through her hair and her fingers disappeared entirely. "It's about intimacy."

"Agreed."

"If the . . . improvising . . . if the improvising makes people more intimate, then it's, like, exploring. Less intimate, then it's just kinky."

The pale-haired woman nipped into her fresh drink. "So you're saying women explore but men are kinky?"

"I'm not kinky," Al Tuschman said.

He had no idea he was going to say it and he could not believe that the words had actually passed his lips. He inhaled sharply, as if to suck them back. An agonizing moment passed. The two friends might ignore him or call him an asshole or simply move away. He tried to look friendly. Not pushy, not leering, not drunk. Above all, not desperate in his loneliness.

The lank-haired woman glanced at him sideways. Blow him off or humor him? She gestured toward him, lifted an eyebrow in what might have been some part of a smile, then turned toward her friend as though she'd proved a point. "You see?"

The thick-haired woman looked away, seemed bothered and hard. Up until that moment, she'd seemed the cuddlier of the two; in fantasy, she'd been the one that Al Tuschman was going to sleep with. Now he realized the light-haired woman was really much more spirited, appealing.

"You see?" she said again. "Not all men are kinky. Some men know what simple pleasure is. No games. No bullshit. Pleasure and comfort. Am I right?"

Al Tuschman sipped his 'Buca, dared now to look full at her, soulful. She had high cheekbones, cat's eyes; the nostrils weren't really so bad. He told himself, Don't say too much, don't try too hard, don't blow it. "For me," he said, "that's what it's always been about."

That was good. He was pleased with that. The lank-haired woman smiled, opened up her shoulders, showed some teeth. He could almost taste her mouth. He stopped himself from reaching out his hand, draping his palm across her wrist. Too bold, too soon.

The thick-haired woman reached forward over the bar and roughly stubbed out her cigarette. She tossed back her vodka like she was ready to leave. Al thought: Good friend, she knows when to get out of the way.

Then she propped her chin in her hand. She fixed Al Tuschman with a stare that cut right through the smoke and through the other woman's gaze, a stare that was half defiant and half imploring. Her lips puckered and breath moved between them in the instant before there was a sound. "Prove it."

Not till he was bending over on the sidewalk to unravel Fifi's leash from the parking meter where she'd been tied did Al Tuschman realize he was very tipsy. Blood rushed to his head, stars burst at the edges of his vision, annexed themselves to the insane glare and flash of Duval Street.

But the thick-haired woman was impressed with and reassured by the little shih tzu. So unlikely, so unmacho. She petted the dog, made faces at it. Then, cuddly once again, she leaned against Al, her side warm along his flank, as they strolled together off Duval and through the quieter streets toward Paradise.

They went through the gate, around the pool that shimmered blue in a mild breeze.

"Nice place," the thick-haired woman said.

Al nodded modestly. "Where you staying?"

"Me? I live here."

Al felt dumb for asking. But impressed with himself too. And flattered. Sleeping with a local. More exciting, memorable, more legit, somehow, than just colliding with another unmoored tourist far away from either person's life.

He unlocked the door of his bungalow. Inside, they had their first kiss, peppery with the taste of her cigarettes.

"I'm glad I'm here with you," she said.

"I'm glad too," said Al.

"You don't talk much, do you?"

"Sometimes I do, sometimes I don't."

"Strong silent type," she said.

"Not really," he admitted. "Sometimes, to the dog, I ramble on and on."

She laughed, and the laugh became a long kiss. They pressed and petted. Loins together. They had their clothes on and they were four feet from the bed. An awkward moment.

"You a little nervous?" the thick-haired woman asked.

Al tried to answer, could only nod.

"I am too. I think that's nice, don't you?"

She led him toward the bed, undid the buttons of his tight blue shirt. Lifted off her loose, thin blouse, stepped out of her soft and draping skirt. He looked at her. She was bluish in the moonlight. Fleshy and candid as the women in the painting on the wall above the bowl of fruit. He kicked off his shoes and wrestled with his pants and pulled back the thin blanket.

She lay down. He was in love with her hair by now. It was so thick and springy that it made a second pillow for her head. He settled in next to her and they embraced. Mouths together; chests together. Kinky? Al thought dimly. Who needed kinky when there was such delight in lips and arms, such unfailing suspense in the surge of bellies and the wrapping of thighs?

That's when he felt the first pinch on his scrotum.

It was a harder pinch than was really necessary. There was a certain excitement in it, though he couldn't honestly say it felt that good.

Then the thick-haired woman made a soft and teasing and catlike sound. It might have been *meow* or maybe only *ow.*

He liked the sound but didn't know just what to make of it. Was she goading him to pinch her in return? Where?

Then she pinched down really hard, so hard that his testicles seemed to flash forth a pulsing red and green like Christmas bulbs.

Through the pain he noticed that both her hands were on his chest.

And her soft and playful *ow* rose to an enraged and screeching *OUCH,* and she belted him across the temple with her forearm.

Wrestling with the bedclothes, thrashing and struggling to free herself, she hissed out, "You're not kinky, you sick bastard? Just one more sick bastard!"

She managed to rise, clutching at the inside of her thigh. As she did so, something clunked onto the floor and seemed to drag itself away. Fifi, her neat paws skidding on the varnished boards, ran in circles until she'd tracked it down. There was a scuffle, then a yelp.

A befuddled but tumescent Alan Tuschman scrambled up from bed. He watched the thick-haired woman quickly climb into her skirt. The anguish of losing her briefly overwhelmed the searing pain in his groin, and it was a heartbeat or two before he focused on the unnatural weight and appalling pressure he was feeling there.

Then he looked down and he screamed. Loudly. He had a two-pound lobster dangling from his nuts. Its antennae were exploring his stomach hair and its tail was curling upward toward his asshole. "Help!"

The thick-haired woman was not inclined to get that close. She pulled her blouse on and turned her back. "You fucking pervert," she said across her shoulder. "I feel sorry for the dog!"

Al reached down and grabbed the two shells of the lobster claw, tried with all his strength to pry them off his scrotum. "You think I had this planned?" he yelled.

There was no reply. The thick-haired woman was out of there. Hadn't even closed the door behind her.

Hopping madly, fighting with the lobster and fondling his dented balls, Al Tuschman stared out at her sudden absence, at the giant philodendrons and the faint blue shimmer of the pool beyond.

TWO

11

In a clean and quiet Long Island suburb, Nicky Scotto climbed out of the bed he shared with his skinny, late-sleeping wife and padded off to the bathroom. He showered and carefully shaved, paying particular attention to the difficult places at the corners of his mouth. Then he found scissors and trimmed the overly luxuriant fringes of his eyebrows.

Standing now in his underwear and knee-high cashmere socks, he buffed his Bruno Maglis till they gleamed. He pulled on a black silk turtleneck and a pearl-gray worsted suit, and headed off for his first morning at his former job, now very temporarily his again.

He didn't have to dress this fancily for work. In fact, it was totally impractical. The thin soles of the loafers barely cleared the streams of fishy ice water that trickled over tile floors toward half-clogged rusty drains. The silk turtleneck didn't keep him warm enough as he made the rounds of reefer trucks and seafood lockers, which steamed a frosty fog when their doors were opened.

Still, he dressed rich because it reflected how he felt. Walking through the clamor and the echoes of the market, making his presence known, waving benignly to the little people in the stalls as they shoveled ice, uncrated octopus, he might have been an old-time duke parading through his village. People called his name. There was a friendliness in it, almost a hurrah, though it was not the friendliness of equals. It was the friendliness of happy subjects, supplicants who were rewarded as long as they paid tribute and obeyed the rules. Pete, Luigi, Tony, Fred—beyond the confines of the market, they would casually make it known that they called Nicky by his name, and this would give them standing in the wider world.

So, quietly thrilled to be back, he did his circuit, shaking hands, slapping backs, then headed down a chilly corridor toward what used to be his office.

An absurd and salty sorrow tweaked him as he neared the door. Not that there was much to have missed about the place. The lighting was lousy and it smelled of fish. The furniture was cold, cheap metal, and the one, dirty window faced out on a loading dock and a mountain of cracked pallets. Still, when he stepped across the pitted threshold and pulled the string that worked the lights, Nicky Scotto felt a pang. He'd been happy here. It wasn't just the money and the power. He'd felt like he was where he ought to be. And if happiness and belonging didn't give someone a claim, what did?

He went to his old desk. On it, in corny frames, stood pictures of Big Al Marracotta's fat wife and ugly, spoiled kids. He flipped them facedown against the metal, buried them under a phone book. He sat in what used to be his chair, and drummed his fingers on the arm, and told himself not to get too comfortable.

He was there only as a fill-in, a pinch hitter; his pal Donnie kept reminding him of that, as gently as he could. Tony Eggs hadn't changed his mind about who should run the market. Carlo Ganucci had been very clear: when Al Marracotta got back from vacation, he would take over once again.

Well, that was life, thought Nicky Scotto. You're up, you're down; you're in, you're out. But he didn't have to like it, and he didn't have to pretend it felt right. Sitting there as Big Al's sub, guest host on the show he used to run—it felt wrong as hell, wrong as a bad clam beginning to break down and spread its poison through his churning gut.

•

Al Tuschman didn't wake up happy.

His tongue was dry and swollen; there was a deep, slow throb where his spine plugged into his brain. He ached between the legs, and couldn't tell how much of the ache had to do with thwarted sex, and how much with the depredations of the lobster. In a feeble attempt to cheer himself, he remembered that most people paid two hundred bucks a night to be here.

He got up from the sweaty sheets, threw water on his face. He collected Fifi, whose nose bore a deep scratch from a flailing claw, and they headed out for breakfast.

As they rounded the blue pool, Al noticed a tangled and inert lump of something at the bottom. Turned out to be a pair of suffocated lobsters, strangled by chlorine. Al felt a moment's thin revenge, followed quickly by remorse. Poor guys. Try to see it their way. Could they help it they were lobsters? They'd survived bizarre adventures, endured the weight and heat of human crotches, then made a bold break for freedom through terrain as dry and foreign as the moon, only to end up in the dread gravity of the sucking drain.

Then he recalled the thick and springy hair of the woman he almost had, and thought, The hell with 'em, let 'em smother.

He passed the office, and the desk clerk called to him in a tone of mock politeness. By now it was war between the two of them. The passive, insolent employee smirking behind a charade of cheerful service. The disgruntled guest whose grumbling would have to ripen into bodily assault if he ever hoped to express his full dissatisfaction.

"Important call for you this morning," said the clerk. He handed Al a slip of paper, serenely confident that it contained bad news.

Al read it and his headache instantly got worse. Sun Motors in Miami. He asked the clerk for the phone.

The clerk moved grudgingly away to eavesdrop.

He heard Al say, "What? . . . Stolen? . . . Hijacked?! . . . What kind of craziness is hijacked? . . . Now, wait a second. I deal with the public too. So let's make sure we have this clear . . . we're not saying *we'll* work it out. We're saying *you'll* work it out. Right?"

Al slammed the phone down, pushed it across the desk in the direction of the clerk hard enough so that its rubber feet squeaked against the varnish. "What the hell kind of town is this?" he said.

The clerk allowed himself a hint of a smile. "Most people find it a very pleasant and relaxing town."

Al ran a hand through his hair. The motion pulled a throb behind it, as if something were stuck and crawling between his scalp and skull. "And another thing," he said. "Someone put lobsters in my room last night."

The clerk fingered the row of studs above his eyebrow. "You mean orchids."

"Whaddya mean, I mean orchids?" Al demanded. "If I meant orchids, I'd say orchids. I'm saying lobsters."

"Lobsters," the clerk said numbly.

"Lobsters," Al repeated. "In my room. Now they're in the pool."

"Mr. Tuschman. You shouldn't put lobsters in the pool."

"I didn't put them in. They ran in. They dove in. They're dead."

The clerk scratched his shaved head.

"And what's this crap about orchids?" Al asked him.

"Orchids?"

"Yeah, orchids. I said lobsters, you said orchids."

"Right. Someone came last night to deliver orchids."

"And you let him in my room?" said Al.

"I didn't let him in your room. He said he'd leave them by the door."

Al Tuschman bit his lip. "This guy, what did he look like?"

The clerk bit his lip too. "He looked like . . . he looked like . . . who remembers? A delivery man. Apron. Paper hat."

Al drummed his fingers on the counter, thought that over. At last he said, "Where I'm from, florists don't wear paper hats and aprons. Seafood guys wear paper hats and aprons."

"Gee," said the clerk, "I never thought of that." He stifled a yawn.

Disgusted, Al Tuschman turned to go. Halfway to the door, he was struck by something else. "Don't you ever leave here?" he asked the clerk. "Don't you ever sleep?"

"Rents are high. Not everyone appreciates," he whined, "just how hard we work."

"Batt'ries included?" asked Big Al Marracotta.

The clerk shrugged then took back the latex gizmo, tried to figure out how to unscrew the base. The gadget was not as technologically advanced as the ones in *Sex Trek,* but it had a raffish design and a certain ingenuity. Katy Sansone rolled her eyes.

"Yeah, batteries are in there," said the clerk. He sniffled, ran a finger under his nose, then added, "Or you can use the crank."

"And the hot water goes in here?" said Al.

"Hot water, margarine, whatever."

"Would feel good, no?" said Al. He'd taken the thing back and was cranking it in Katy's direction so that it wiggled like a spastic cobra.

"Al," she said, "isn't it a little early?"

In fact they'd just had breakfast. The porn store had been open fifteen minutes. The clerk's first cup of coffee still stood on a display case filled with ticklers and extenders and things with leather straps.

"All of a sudden you're inhibited?" Big Al teased. He flashed that surprising boy-devil grin, the grin that moved his hair and showed the small gap in his teeth. "Like *amore*'s only for the dark of night?"

"I guess I didn't realize it was *amore,*" she said. "Seemed more like Roto-Rooter. I'm going to the beach."

"The beach?" he said. "We been through that."

"Right," said Katy. "You don't like sand and riffraff. So you go to the pool. I'll see you in a couple hours."

Big Al fidgeted, took a moment to decide if he was mad. He felt a little silly with the pleasure unit in his hand and his girl-friend leaning toward the door. Plus, he didn't like her tone. A little bratty and ungrateful. Then again, some spunk, some spirit—it kept things fresh, a little bit on edge. "Fine," he said at last. "I'll see ya later."

Half surprised to be sprung, afraid that Al might quickly change his mind, she pivoted on her tall shoes and bolted from the store.

Breaking out into the clean, hot sunshine of the sidewalk, she inhaled the smells of softening asphalt and sunblock spiced with coconut, and realized all at once that she hadn't had a moment to herself in days. Just to walk at her own pace; to look at what she chose to look at; to breathe.

She walked fast for half a block, as though pursued, then started to relax. Slowing, using her own eyes, she saw and did small things that exhilarated her beyond all proportion to their actual significance. Twirled a postcard rack; smiled at plump twins in a stroller. Took a color brochure from a young woman hawking snorkel trips; listened hungrily as she rhapsodized about coral and striped fish. Paused at a booth promoting sunset sails, and let herself imagine that someday she would be aboard a sailboat. Why not? If she were on her own? Or had a friend to travel with?

Or was with a different sort of man?

There, she'd thought it. For a moment it felt great to think it, but then the feeling backfired, and she felt disloyal, guilty. Un-deserving. How shallow could you get? Three minutes out of Big Al's grasp, and already she was fantasizing life without him. After him. Like he'd died. While she was still riding on his ticket, blowing his money, sharing his bed. It was wrong.

Then again, what was wrong with wanting to be treated right?

Okay, she thought—she'd made certain choices, choices that she wasn't very proud of. Well, so what? Did that mean she was disqualified forever from a little happiness, a little dignity? Wasn't she allowed at least to wonder if there were still men in the world who weren't married, and weren't outlaws, and weren't maniacs? Men who might see in her something more than a sex toy to be visited by other sex toys?

She strolled past T-shirt shops and jewelry stores and new construction. She wished she could do life over; then quickly shuddered at how much trouble that would be; then admitted with something like relief that there was nothing to be done except to go from here.

At an open stand she leaned across a cool chrome counter and ordered up an ice cream cone—vanilla with chocolate jimmies. Her mouth watered as she watched it being made, and she licked it happily as any kid as she headed toward the beach, wondering how long she could dare to stretch these clean, empty hours that were her own.

12

Squid Berman, happy and fulfilled, had just awakened from a beautiful and long night's sleep.

He'd needed it. Two nights ago he'd hardly rested, then he'd done an endless stakeout across the street from Paradise. He'd still been there, skulking in the buttonwood hedge, when Big Al and the thick-haired woman wobbled home together from the bar. He was still there some fifteen minutes later, when the woman, furious and suddenly sober, stormed right out again.

Now he was leaning on a pointy elbow, underneath a tortured sheet, and telling Chop about it.

"Ya shoulda seen the kisser on 'er!" he was saying. "Freaked or what? A masterstroke! I ruined it for 'im, Chop. I ruined it for 'im good."

Chop couldn't get that excited about it. Wacko mischief that no longer involved cars. He was thinking about the silver Lexus. Rip out the seats and you had a fine vehicle. He scratched his neck. Something was making him irritable. Probably that it was clearer all the time that Squid was enjoying this gig a whole lot more than he was. Grudgingly he said, "So what next?"

Squid thought. Thinking made his mouth water; he swallowed and his bony Adam's apple shuttled up and down his neck. Truth was, he didn't know what next, knew only that it had to top what he had done so far. This was the unremitting pressure on the artist, the thing a lunk like Chop would never understand. "Jeez," he said, "lemme savor this one for a while."

"Isn't time," said Chop.

Squid frowned. He knew the other man was right. There was never time. The next hurdle was always in your face before your feet had even reconnected with the ground.

Without getting out of bed, the bandy man bore down, started thinking once again. His eyes bulged, water pooled beneath his tongue, and he dug deeper into the cackling mysteries of making someone miserable.

Big Al Marracotta strolled back to the Conch House weighed down with two big bags of goodies. He had probes and plungers, harnesses and clips, lingerie and jellies. He had extra batteries and a video shot entirely from underneath a glass coffee table. He was ready for more vacation.

But back at his hotel, with Katy gone and nothing else to do, he let his mind flit just briefly to his business. In truth it had been days since he'd thought at all about fish and payoffs, ice and trucks, no-show jobs and haulers' kickbacks and soggy cartons full of halibut and crab. Now a sudden nameless qualm made him feel that he should check in, at least, see how things were going.

He put the goodies by the TV set and sat down on the edge of his giant bed to place a call to Benny Franco, the guy he'd left in charge.

This was a somewhat complicated procedure. There was a phone in the fish market office, but it was used only for the most mundane chitchat with outsiders. Real business calls were routed through a pay phone bolted to the loading dock across the yard. This meant that an underling would have to take the call, determine if it was worth a bigger man's attention, then trudge through slush and slime to fetch the boss. The boss, in turn, would have to put his topcoat on, his scarf, and tiptoe through the oily puddles.

Sitting there in Florida, Big Al remembered how freezing cold the receiver usually was against his ear. He dialed.

In Manhattan a guy picked up the phone, said, "Yeah?"

"Lemme talk ta Benny."

The request made the underling suspicious. Everyone who mattered knew that Benny wasn't there no more, had been led away in handcuffs. He said, "Benny ain't here. Who's iss?"

"Who's iss?!" said Al, and put a little menace in it. "Who's *iss*?"

"Lefty."

"Lefty, you putz. It's Al. Go get Benny."

Lefty hesitated. He was a cautious guy and not good at explaining things. He knew there was no percentage in carrying bad news. He said simply, "Hey, Al. Hol' on a minute."

He left the phone dangling like a hanged cat and trudged through the slush and slime to fetch Nicky.

"Who is it?" Nicky wanted to know before bothering with the topcoat and the scarf.

Lefty didn't want to say the name. No percentage setting up a meet between two guys who were never gonna like each other. "I think y'oughta take it" was all he said.

Nicky slid into his coat and stepped outside. The yard stank of diesel fumes and fish. Gross water seeped into his loafers. He picked up the phone, which was achingly cold against his ear. "Yeah?"

On his giant Key West bed, Big Al Marracotta yanked in his eyebrows so that his salt-and-pepper helmet crawled. Benny's voice he knew. "You ain't Benny."

"Did I fucking say I was Benny? All I said was yeah. Who's iss?"

Big Al puffed up a little, gave his neck a twist. Whoever this guy was, he didn't like his tone. "This is your boss, asshole."

The words chafed Nicky badly. Boss? Big Al? He said, "I ain't aware I got a boss."

The insolence, in turn, made Big Al wary; he did not want to admit that he had no idea who he was talking to. He wiggled his butt against the sheets and decided to seek more information. "Where the fuck is Benny?"

Nicky stomped his feet to keep the blood from freezing and tried to have a little fun. "How's the weather down in Flahda?"

"Fuckin' gorgeous."

Nicky thought about Chop and Squid, who were costing him several grand a day to make this guy's life a living hell. "And things are goin' good?"

"Beautiful," said Al.

Nicky smiled to think he must be lying through his teeth. Sure he was. Nobody ever admitted that vacation turned out lousy.

Al had finally put two and two together. "This Nicky?"

"Bingo."

"Fuck you doin' there?"

"Runnin' the place, that's all."

"Where's Benny?"

"Prob'ly at his lawyer's," Nicky said. "You picked a loser, Al. Benny got indicted."

Al sprang off the bed and pirouetted. Wistfully, he looked across the room at his trove of unsampled sex toys. "Shit. I'm comin' home."

"Don't let it fuck up your vacation, Al."

"I'll be there tomorra."

"Al, hey, market's inna best hands it could be in. Best hands ever. Least that's Tony Eggs' opinion."

Nicky was pleased with that remark, so pleased that for a moment he forgot how cold he was.

Al said, "Yeah? So why'd he kick you out and make you one more pissant onna street again?"

Nicky shivered. "Listen, pal—"

"I'm coming home," said Al. "I'm calling Tony."

Nicky shuffled his stinging feet. Too late he understood that his ballbusting was utterly misfiring. He should have made nice, been reassuring. Now he would be shortchanged even in his brief, false tenure back on top. His voice took on a wheedling tone that galled him, and he tried to patch things up. "Al, hey, don't get your bowels in an uproar. I'm just kiddin' with ya. Everything's fine. I'm just fillin' in. Temporary, like."

In Key West, Big Al Marracotta paced to the limits of the phone cord and considered. "I'll check that with Tony, Carlo."

"Yeah, okay, check," said Nicky, his voice still more conciliatory and chagrined. Bending over just to have a few more days in charge, pretending.

Al Marracotta hung up in his ear.

Nothing was more bitter than knowing that you'd lost after thinking that you'd won. Nicky Scotto stared at the phone a couple seconds, like he was blaming it for how things went. He slapped his arms for warmth, wiggled toes inside his squishy shoes, and trudged back through the oily puddles to what used to be his office.

13

Nothing stays strange for long. Normal is what's there.

Al Tuschman sat out by the pool at Paradise and looked around. Bare-breasted lesbians with boxer shorts and hairy armpits. Sleek gay men glistening like basted ducks in Chinatown. The Eurotrash ménage à trois with their stacks of fashion magazines, their ceaseless chattering and giggling. So what else was new?

Al was getting to feel so blithe that he seriously considered getting naked. Told himself it wasn't prudishness that held him back, but concern that his dented and distended scrotum would appear deformed, grotesque. He promised himself he'd strip as soon as the tortured sac resumed its accustomed shape and size.

In the meantime he tanned. At the very least, he would go home brown and make other people jealous. He lay back on his lounge and offered up his face. Hot sun scratched at his hairline and seared right through his eyelids.

It was pleasant for a little while. But Al was dark to begin with and tanned easily. No challenge; not a mission. He was soon bored.

He sat up, then stood. Light-headed, he blinked until the colors returned to flesh and flowers, and decided he would go check out the beach. He put on sandals, fetched a shirt that sort of matched his bathing trunks, and put Fifi on the leash. He got directions from the drowsy and mock-helpful clerk behind the desk and headed out.

The walk was a great deal longer than he'd been led to believe. Still, it wasn't long enough for him to notice the Jaguar that crawled along amid the traffic of rented convertibles and whining mopeds and clunky bikes, now lolling half a block behind him, now pulling ahead, then discreetly circling back.

Al's route wound through town streets full of bars and fishing stores, past a misplaced brick enclave of courthouses and county offices, through an apartment complex whose faux-Bahamian motif was the only thing that prevented it from looking just like Jersey. Beyond the complex was a half-abandoned navy base penned in by a rusting chain-link fence, and past the bunkers and scrap heaps of the base was a narrow road that finally got sandy at its edges.

Along this road, his throat parched, his headache returning, and his heels beginning to blister, Al Tuschman saw someone he vaguely recognized.

She was moving toward him on silver high-heeled sandals. She was long-legged, slim-hipped, and bosomy, with a rather small-featured face behind big sunglasses, topped by raven hair that salt air and dyes had made a little stiff and spiky.

Their eyes met, then tried to slide politely apart but stuck, as happens between people who look half familiar. Al finally remembered where and when he'd seen her. Breakfast yesterday. Promenading with a short guy. "Hey, there," he said. "Where's your dog?"

Katy could not help frowning at the mention of the slobbering and thankless rottweiler. "Oh, hi," she said. "It's not my dog, it's my boyfriend's."

She regretted the words before she was finished saying them, but there it was, she'd said them. Why did she do that to herself? Fact one: I have a boyfriend. A possessive, maniac boyfriend who takes care of everything and holds me back from anything decent while I play right along.

Al had to say something, so he said, "Ah. How's the beach?"

"Nice," she said. "Once you get to it. Water's really green. Wonder why that is?"

Al wished he knew. He shrugged. The Jag squeezed past them on the narrow pavement, considerately slowing as it headed toward the beach. Its effect was to push them to the margin of the road, moving them closer together.

The woman crouched to pet the shih tzu. It was a long way down for her but she descended very smoothly, ankles and knees and waist compacting like a closed expansion gate. To the creature she said, "And what's your name?"

"Fifi," Al told her.

"Fifi," she repeated, rubbing the shih tzu's knobby head.

"Mine's Al," he volunteered.

She kept her face down and gave a quick and mordant chuckle. "So's his." The disembodied pronoun sounded strange, and then again it didn't. It was the way unhappy people referred to their partner when their partner seemed less like a person than a blank but overwhelming fact. Almost as an afterthought, she said, "Mine's Katy."

She straightened up. She was nice and tall. Her forehead was as high as Al's nose. She leaned forward like she was ready to start walking. Al hoped that she would stay a little bit. "You having fun down here?" he asked her.

"Pretty nice," she said. "You?"

He thought a moment, scratched his ear. Then he said, "Not really."

This was so wildly and gauchely honest that both of them held their breath a heartbeat, then let out a giggle. No one ever admitted that vacation was going lousy.

Laughing was a great relief, a godsend, so Al went on. "I'm staying at this weird place. Paradise, it's called."

"Not exactly modest," Katy said.

"No. And like, weird stuff has been happening to me from the minute I arrived."

"They say Key West is like that."

"No, I mean really weird," Al said.

"Okay," she gave in. "How weird?"

"Like someone filled my car with calamari. Then someone put lobsters in my bed."

Katy's eyes screwed down behind her sunglasses. She figured he was bullshitting but she didn't see the harm. "You must have some wild and crazy friends."

"I don't have a friend within a thousand miles," Al said. He said it a little louder than he meant to, and the words seemed to hollow out a lonely capsule in the air.

Katy didn't see it as lonely. She saw it as free and exotic and bold. "You often travel alone?"

"Depends." Depended on whether he had a girlfriend when he won a selling contest, which usually he didn't, in part because he spent so many evenings on the selling floor.

"I bet," said Katy, "that's really when you see great stuff, when you get to do exactly what you want."

Al pursed his lips. "If you can figure what that is."

"Me," she said, "I'd go out on a sailboat, look at coral, look at fish."

Al finished his own thought. "And, like, if no one steals your car."

"Your car got stolen too?"

He nodded, shrugged.

She gave her head a sympathetic though not totally persuaded shake, then began to move away. She didn't really want to move away, but they were strangers, and she had a boyfriend, and what else was there to do? "Well, I hope things go better here on in."

"Couldn't go worse," said Al. He looked for some wood to knock. There weren't any trees along the narrow road. He wished he hadn't said it.

They moved off in opposite directions. After a few steps Al looked back across his shoulder. He'd had a fantasy that the tall woman was looking at him too.

She was not, of course. She was going back to the man who'd brought her here.

Al continued toward the beach. Without admitting he was doing it, he counted up the days until vacation would be over and he could go back home. In the meantime he looked forward to the yielding crunch of sand and the cooling sting of ocean water against his blistered feet.

14

From where the road finally ended, it was another third of a mile to the water's edge. Through a scorching asphalt parking lot. Beyond a grove of Australian pines whose feathery needles imperfectly screened the blaze of mid-afternoon sun, and where dog and master drank greedily from a lukewarm fountain. Down a slope of coral rocks that challenged ankles and clawed at heels. Then past a swath of trucked-in sand that gave, at last, onto the ocean.

By the time he got there, Al Tuschman was really ready for a swim.

Squid Berman had figured that he might be.

He'd stationed himself—in a loud and baggy print bathing suit that came down to his knees, bug-eyed goggles, and a pebbled shower cap—in a shadowed cranny of a pile of rocks that rose up from the green water thirty, forty yards offshore. Kids with snorkels climbed up on the rocks, yipping like a pack of seals. But Squid's weirdness enforced an empty space around him, and from his private grotto he had a panoramic view of the life on land—the gay trysting grounds over near the jetty, the picnic area with its whorls of charcoal smoke, the occasional topless European with teenage boys walking casually back and forth around her.

He saw Big Al swagger toward the shoreline, his water-shy dog quailing behind, sniffing sand. Watched as he kicked off his sandals and stepped into the first cool lick of the ocean. He imagined he heard a sizzle come off the tough guy's feet.

He willed him in farther, deeper.

But Al Tuschman stayed right where he was. He still had his shirt on, his sunglasses. The water felt great but he wasn't sure how much of it he wanted. He was an okay swimmer, not terrific. Besides, it was a commitment, going in the ocean. The adjustment in body temperature. The inevitable dried salt itching in the chest hair. The wet bathing suit that was sure to chafe the inner thighs on the long walk home.

Then again, there was the widely known effect of cool water on the scrotum. Given his stretched and irritated state, it might be very therapeutic. He pulled off his sweaty shirt, laid it on the sand with his sandals and his shades, told Fifi to be good and stay right where she was.

Squid Berman watched him stride into the ocean, big legs fighting off the suck of sand and the weight of water. Squinting through his goggles, he firmed his concentration and thought, Come on, you bastard, dive. Swim!

Al Tuschman took his time. Strolled in up to his calves, his knees. Stared off at fishing boats returning to the harbor, pleasure sloops just heading out. Felt the faint and ghostly pull of an undertow that was stifled by the reef.

Finally a wavelet lapped against his bathing suit and wet his nuts. The water wasn't cold but still he shivered. Ravaged skin contracted, inhaled into corrugations. He rose up on tiptoe, did a little dance.

The crisis over, he took another step, feeling now a primordial delight and wondering, as people always did, why he'd hesitated plunging in. A resolute stride brought the water past his waist, and he made a less than graceful lunge that soaked his head and started him swimming toward the far horizon.

Crouched in his cranny of the rockpile, Sid the Squid swallowed hard, licked dried salt from his twitching lips.

Al swam ten strokes, twenty, scudding even with, then past,

the outcrop. The exercise chased away the remnants of his hangover. Not as fit as he wished he were, he yet reveled in the strength of his arms, the scissoring force of his kick. The ocean blotted out sound, turned the searing sun into a gentle blanket tickling his back, and it dimly dawned on Al that, for the first time since he'd got here, he felt like he was on vacation. Away from everything, including his usual self. Refreshed by strangeness. Not so much feeling as being the plain, gut happiness that some people insisted was a mission. Joyfully, he swam another dozen strokes.

Then he saw the shark.

The shark was around the same size he was, but half of it was mouth. Behind the fearsome maw was a rank of gill slits like the airholes on old Buicks, and behind the gill slits a miraculous machinery of fin and muscle that gave swimming the suave weightlessness of flight.

The beast was fifteen, twenty feet ahead of Al, swimming slowly with fluid wiggles, crosswise to him. Al fixed on one beady, sleepily malicious eye and froze. His body lost its buoyancy, helplessly went vertical. His feet groped for, and couldn't find, the bottom. He held his breath, treaded water, and watched.

It seemed the shark was easing past him. Then it turned. Maybe it had caught a glint of pinky ring. It banked with the merest flick of fin and tail, and torpedoed straight toward Al. Its mouth was slightly open, crooked rows of incurved teeth just barely visible. In the instant before he screamed, Al imagined he saw water sluicing through the gills.

He screamed before his face was quite clear of the ocean. He sucked in a mouthful of water and choked on the stony taste of salt.

Still spluttering, he swam like hell for land, arms thrashing, neck craning. Even as he kicked he tried to pull his legs into his torso, hiding his feet and knees from the ripping pull of triangle teeth.

Terror made him forget about the need to breathe; he was winded after half a dozen strokes. For a while, fear filled in for oxygen, and he kept pumping with his arms although his ears were ringing and his vision had narrowed into a hellish tube of glare.

He was even with the rockpile when he saw that the shark had changed its course, had circled up ahead of him. Had cut him off from other swimmers the way a lion cuts from the herd a single antelope. Was blocking the salvation of the beach and forcing him seaward once again.

Al skidded against the scant resistance of the water, begged his body to pivot, somersaulted outbound. His lungs burned; his arms screamed in their sockets. Confused and piteous thoughts raced through his mind: the orphaned Fifi, never knowing what terrible thing she'd done to be abandoned on the beach. Old Mr. Kleiman with his opal tie tack, standing on an ottoman to eulogize his favorite salesman . . . He swam, waiting each moment for the clamping bite and the nauseating rend of flesh, the iron smell of his own blood spilling in the ocean. He couldn't tell if he was crying or if his eyes were simply melting into the salt water.

Ahead of him the blank and bright horizon was suddenly sealed off by the gray flank of the shark.

It had circled once again, bands of muscle folding back upon themselves with humiliating ease. The red cave of the open mouth was like a door to hell. Once again Al did a desperate one-eighty. His arms would no longer lift clear of the water; he paddled like a hound dog throwing dirt. His hip joint scraped, his pumping legs abraded sinew with each kick.

Sucking spasmodically at the soup of air and water, his lungs heavy and puffed up like a mildewed sponge, he flailed toward the impossibly distant shore. Flailed until his sinking feet miraculously touched bottom.

Leaning forward on numb hands and jelly knees, droplets flying from his heaving chest, he rose up and stomped through the cruel knobs of coral that floored the last fringe of the ocean, escaping at last from the horrors of the sea and collapsing full-length on the beach like a shipwrecked, sun-mad sailor.

Fifi ran over and licked his face. He turned on his side and burped up salt water, gurgling and wheezing as he strained to breathe.

In the shadow of his rock, Squid Berman's brain was itching underneath the shower cap, his eyes tearing with squelched laughter inside their glinting goggles. He fiddled with the radio control and steered the toy shark back to him, then pulled the little air plug and deflated it at leisure in the privacy of his grotto. No one but Big Al had seen a thing.

The tough guy writhed on the beach a couple minutes, coughing, spitting. Then he sat up, shaking his head, groping for his sunglasses.

When he finally stood up on shaky legs to leave, Squid noted with satisfaction that he was too freaked even to go to the water's edge to rinse off the coarse and salty sand that coated him from feet to cheek.

15

Katy Sansone knew what she would find when she returned to the Conch House.

She'd find Big Al either sprawled out on a poolside lounge or chest-deep at the swim-up bar. Either way, he'd have had a couple drinks. That boy-devil look would be stretching the corners of his eyes, and he'd be getting horny. He'd make some teasing cracks to stoke himself along. Ask her if she got picked up by any bulging Cuban studs at the beach. Offer comments on the breasts and backsides of the women at the pool. It would all be flip and crude—and also, Katy could not help but admit, comforting in its familiarity. Al had his routines. He was predictable. A man in whom habits cut an instant groove. Blunt in his wants, consistent in his appetites. And, no matter what else was right or wrong or crazy or impossible, it was nice to be consistently desired.

So she was surprised and, in spite of herself, a little disappointed when he wasn't where she thought he'd be. She walked the whole perimeter of the pool, skirted the lanai rooms, the towel kiosk. Scanned the flushed and vacant faces at the bar. No Al. She took a moment to decide what she should do. His absence, she felt, gave her permission to go off on her own a little longer. That might be nice, and yet . . . and yet she sort of didn't want to. This embarrassed her. Did it mean, she wondered, that she actually missed the sonofabitch? Or only that she'd had all the independence she could handle for one day?

She went up to their room, found Al in the same long pants he'd been wearing when they parted. He was pacing between the TV and the window, and his expression wasn't playful. Katy's first thought was that she'd stayed away too long and he was mad. She waited for him to talk.

"How was the beach?" he asked. He said it with neither interest nor blame, and Katy felt relieved.

"Fine. Nice," she said. No reason to elaborate, since he wasn't listening. She watched him pace. The skin was drawn and gray around his eyebrows, the stubble on his chin was flecked with silver, and she realized that he truly wasn't young. Not young, not happy all the time, not free of worries and responsibilities. "Something wrong?" she asked.

Big Al paused in his circuit, briefly stared up at her. The question gave him a dilemma. You didn't talk to broads. That was elementary. But up North he would have had pals, goombahs, that he could bitch to. Here there was no one else, and keeping silent gave rise to stomach acid. Laconically, he said, "Guy I left in charge . . . aw, it's all fucked up."

The answer, in turn, put Katy in doubt as to how much further she should go. Left in charge of what? She pretty much knew that Al was Mafia. He carried guns and knives and large amounts of cash; his New York friends all talked like they were eating crackers. But as to the specifics of his business, she was serenely in the dark. She had noticed that, when they dined out in the city, it was almost always seafood, and Al got fawned over shamelessly. The best tables. Free champagne. But that was as much as she knew. Now she tried to steer a middle course between showing concern and seeming to pry. "Fucked up how?" she asked.

Al was wearing a loose-fitting shirt, but he twisted his neck like his collar was too tight. Fighting back each word, he grunted, "Guy they replaced my guy wit'—worst guy they coulda picked."

Katy sat down on the bed, tried not to notice the two big bags of sex toys leaning up against the television cabinet. "How come?"

"How come what?" said Al, his throat closing down around the rising question.

"How come he's the worst guy?"

"'Cause we hate each other's guts."

"Why?"

"Why?" Al echoed, and stopped to ponder. Up until that moment it hadn't dawned on him that there had to be a reason. "He hates me," he said at last, "'cause he thinks I took his job away. And I hate him 'cause he hates me."

Katy said, "If that's the only—"

Big Al, suddenly impatient, annoyed with himself for blabbing, waved his arms, started pacing once again. "I don't wanna talk no more," he said. "What I said, fuhget about it."

Katy watched him pace, the short legs seeming disconnected from the barrel chest, the skin of the face pulled back taut as that of an astronaut. He went from carefree to wretched with almost nothing in between, and Katy had to acknowledge that his seldom-seen unhappiness gave a new dimension to his carnality, made of it a kind of victory. He stole pleasure between fits of misery. The pleasure had to be as extreme as his anxieties, and his greed for it was in proportion to his desperation. Knowing in some corner of her being that she was being suckered, was suckering herself, she felt a surge of tenderness for her thug of a boyfriend. He had his problems too. "Hey, Al," she said. "How 'bout a back rub?"

"A back rub?" he said, and he gave a little snort. The snort was not derisive, just surprised. A back rub. A simple kindness. Unselfish. "Katy," he said, "you're really a good kid."

"Come on," she said, and motioned him off his circuit to the bed.

He threw himself facedown at her feet.

She got up on her knees and worked his knotty shoulders. He

moaned, he sighed, and after a few minutes, not really meaning it but feeling it was called for by the moment, he said, "I don't deserve a girlfriend good as you."

Powered by a stubborn reflex sympathy, she leaned into his flank and vaguely wondered why it was so hard for her to accept that he was absolutely right.

The knots were somewhat letting go until the phone rang.

But at the first clang of the instrument they came cramping back all along his spine. Big Al quickly scrambled onto his side and told Katy maybe she'd like to take a bath. He didn't pick up the receiver until she'd closed the bathroom door behind her and started water running.

Then he finally squeezed the thing and said hello.

"Al? Carlo."

He knew it would be Carlo. He'd tried to reach the *consigliere* an hour or so before. It took the frail old guy about that long to drain his silty bladder and shuffle to a safe phone he could use.

Now Big Al got straight to the point. "What's this bullshit Nicky's in charge?"

"Someone's gotta be in charge," said Carlo calmly.

"Why him?"

"Who else is there, Al?"

Big Al knew this argument, and for him it didn't wash. Sure, the ranks had thinned. Sure, it was tough to find a colleague who was halfway competent and not in jail. But it wasn't *that* tough. "Come on," he said. "There's Rod the Cod. There's Big Tuna Calabro. Guys I trust. Guys I can talk to, for Chrissake."

Carlo didn't answer. Air wheezed through his nose.

"Somethin' else is goin' on," Al said.

Carlo came forth with a soft and weary sigh. "Don't make more a this than what's there."

"So what's there?" pressed Al Marracotta.

Ganucci sniffled, said at last, "Al, ya want the trut'?"

"Nah, I want more bullshit."

"I think Tony's p.o.'d ya took vacation."

Al sprang up from the bed, wrapped himself in phone cord. "P.o.'d I took vacation? This is fuckin' rich. Once every t'ree, four years a guy can't go off wit' a broad a lousy week or so? This is fuckin' America, Carlo!"

"I'm not takin' a position," the *consigliere* purred. "You asked what's goin' on, I gave you my opinion."

Big Al thought that over. He hoped that thinking would calm him down, but for him it didn't work that way. "So lemme get this straight," he said. "I'm forty-six years old. I been workin' wit' you people thirty years. An' I'm bein' punished, like a fuckin' kid, for goin' on vacation?"

"Al, don't look at it like—"

"I mean, if Tony wants me so bad to be home, he can't call me, man to man, and ask me ta come back?"

"He doesn't want you to come home," the *consigliere* said. He said it softly, and he meant it to be soothing, though of course Al heard it just the opposite. Defiance and insecurity were insepa- rable in Big Al. You couldn't tell him what to do and you couldn't tell him you didn't much care what he did.

He said, "That preening fuck Nicky's doin' my job, and Tony doesn't want me to come home?"

Ganucci sighed. These logical tangles—they happened more and more as he got older, and he never quite knew where the con- fusion started. "Al, he'd love to have you home. Tell ya what. I think I got it, a way that everybody's happy: have vacation, *then* come home."

Stubbornly, Al said, "Like I could be happy, this bullshit goin' on?"

"Al," the *consigliere* urged, "relax—"

"Well, I'm gonna be happy," Big Al insisted, his feisty side once more rearing up to defeat his paranoia. He thought about Katy, naked in a fragrant bath. He glanced off at his brand-new stash of gizmos. "I'm gonna have a fuckin' cabaret."

He almost knew that he was lying. His body was still in Florida, there was still sunshine and champagne and sex, but his vacation was basically over, and in the pit of his stomach he knew it. Nicky Scotto, after all, had succeeded brilliantly in spoiling it for him, if not quite in the manner he'd intended.

"Fine, Al, fine," said Carlo Ganucci. His bladder was burning and he wanted at all costs to end this no-win conversation. "Have a great time and come home when you're ready. We'll be thrilled to have you back. Goo'bye."

16

Lungs sodden, legs heavy and chafed, Al Tuschman trudged slowly back toward his hotel. Salt simmered in his belly; he coughed if he drew air too deep into his chest. Late sun baked his back, and he was barely aware of Fifi tugging at her leash, urging him along the sandy road between the navy's chain-link fences.

He was thinking about his luck.

There were perhaps two dozen people in the water near where he'd been swimming. Why had the shark selected him to chase? For that matter, why had some crazy, tourist-hating vandal picked his car to trash? And what about the freak hijacking? And what about the faceless delivery man putting lobsters in his bed?

Coincidence? Up until that moment he'd assumed so; his misfortunes had come too thick and fast for him to think about them in any other way. Luck, after all, good or bad, was famously streaky. He'd seen that on the selling floor, the ballfield.

But there were limits to what could be ascribed to luck alone, and now, finally, it dawned on Alan Tuschman that perhaps there was some other cause for his misfortunes. A pattern. The shark, okay, that was an act of God. But the other disasters— they were bizarre, ridiculous, but maybe there was a pattern to them nonetheless.

He pondered as he strolled. Was someone mad at him? He ran a catalog of those he might have wronged. Salesmen were not above exaggerating the merits of their wares—might there be a seriously disgruntled and deranged customer lurking out there somewhere? Possible; not likely. His ex? She was happily remarried, their relation cordial though distant. For better or worse, there were no scorned women in his recent past, still less jealous husbands. Who then?

Strolling now along streets lined with hibiscus shrubs and shaded by enormous banyans, he scanned his conscience and found it basically clear. He was an okay guy, not a saint, but a person of average virtue, ordinary decency. He was gentle with animals and would return a wallet if he found one. Essentially honest. Peaceable. Preferring to be kind than otherwise.

Such people were supposed to be rewarded. By God, or the universe, or however you wanted to put it. If not with gaudy gifts, then at least with neutral fortune and peace of mind. This Al had been taught, and this he still believed.

So why did he have less peace of mind than he'd had three days ago? Either the universe was out of whack, or he was looking at it wrong.

The universe, he couldn't fix. So he finessed his point of view.

These calamities that kept happening to him—maybe they weren't what they seemed. He'd been seeing himself as chosen victim, singled out for misery—but maybe that was a mistake. This unlikely, pinpoint malice that found him time and time again—maybe the real intention was something altogether different.

He walked, he pondered, then suddenly it hit him.

Hit him so abruptly that he laughed out loud from the bottom of his burning lungs. Of course! Of course that's what it was! No one was out to get him. He wasn't targeted for torment after all. A great wave of relief swept warmly over him, coupled with humble amusement that he hadn't caught on, solved the riddle sooner. He shook his head, and laughed some more, and wiped his eyes, and his dog looked back at him across her shoulder as though he'd lost his mind.

"Nicky," said his friend Donnie Falcone, "don't even think about it."

"How can I not think about it?" Nicky said, fingering the collar of his turtleneck.

In New York it was already dusk, one of those brown dusks that buries a gray day with people barely noticing the fade. They were having a cocktail in Tribeca. This was no dim and somber Mob joint but a hip place with an artist or two crammed in among the brokers. The waiter for their miniature table was skinny and wore black. There were women at the bar with straight, lank hair and bags under their eyes. Donnie, lean and lugubrious in his big black coat, almost looked like he belonged.

"I'm there," Nicky Scotto went on, "I'm runnin' things again—how can I not think about it?"

Donnie rubbed his long and concave face. "Find a way," he urged. "Be practical, Nicky. Skim your twenty, thirty, whatever you can manage in a week, and let it go."

"Twenty, thirty," Nicky said dismissively. "It's not about the money."

Donnie sipped his martini. "Don't make me laugh, I got chap lips."

"Okay, it's not just about the money. It's about who's the right guy—"

Donnie was rolling his cocktail napkin up around the damp base of his glass. "Nicky," he broke in, "lemme ask you somethin'. How'd you get the job?"

Nicky leaned in closer across the table that was barely big enough to hold two sets of elbows. "I tol' ya. Tony decided—"

"Fuhget Tony decided. How did you actually get the job? Who tol' you you had it?"

"Carlo," Nicky admitted. "Carlo called me up—"

"Exactly," Donnie said. "Carlo. Not Tony. Carlo. Zat tell you anything?"

Nicky looked stubborn in his bafflement.

"Here's what it tells me," his friend went on. "It tells me that who runs the fish market for one lousy week is exactly the kinda piddly bullshit that Tony don't wanna be bothered havin' a sit-down about."

"But if I just explain to him—"

"Explain what? Look, you want my advice, here it is: fuhget about lookin' ta sit down wit' Tony."

Nicky pouted, chased condensation down to the bottom of his glass of scotch. "Ta you it's piddly bullshit," he complained. "Ta me it's like a whole new chance."

"Fine. Except it isn't."

"How you know it isn't?" Nicky challenged. "How you know it isn't a tryout, like, a test."

Donnie raised his neat hands in surrender. "Okay, okay, I don't know nothin'. I only know that Tony's gonna be aggravated, ya waste his time wit' this."

"Waste his time? It's an opportu—"

"Nicky, you're makin' a mistake."

Nicky Scotto, annoyed but not dissuaded, gestured for another round of drinks. The waiter, more than cool, answered the gesture with the most elegant of tiny nods, and wove toward them through the crowded place as silent as a fish.

Al Tuschman was still chortling off and on when he walked into the office of Paradise and asked to use the phone. He was flushed and disheveled, and the desk clerk with the eyebrow studs looked at him with politely smiling disapproval.

"Been drinking, Mr. Tuschman?"

"Only half the ocean. If you'll excuse me, this is gonna be long distance."

He dialed, leaning on the counter. The clerk moved off just to the edge of earshot.

Waiting for the call to be picked up, Al got giddy once again. It's what happened when a man was allowed to crawl back from the precipice. Relief became a species of dementia. His chest heaved, his nose ran, and when Moe Kleiman finally lifted the phone and said a friendly, salesmanlike hello, Al had no breath to speak.

"Hello?" his employer said again. "Hello? Kleiman Brothers Furniture."

"You guys," Al Tuschman managed between snorts. "What a buncha kibitizers!"

"Who is this?" asked his boss.

Al wheezed through soggy passages. "The lobsters. The calamari. Jesus, howdya manage?"

"Al?"

"Really had me goin'. Thought . . . Christ, I don't know what I thought."

"If this is Al—"

"And about the car, I mean, jeez, the trip was prize enough. Ya didn't have to glom the car—"

"What car?"

"—pay off the lease—"

"Are you *meshuga* altogether?"

"Come on, Mr. Kleiman. Joke's over. Time to let it go."

"Are you okay, Al? Let what go?"

Al hesitated, cleared his throat of salt. Belatedly, it dawned on him that he must be sounding like a lunatic. He tried to cling to his giddiness, which was also his hope, but it was going, fast; emptily he watched it slip away like a loved one at the airport. Desperate now, he said, "Really, Mr. Kleiman, about these pranks—"

"Pranks? Al, trust me, I don't know what you're talking about. Is something wrong?"

He struggled for a normal breath and strove now for a sober tone. "Wrong? Oh, no. Coupla funny things have happened. I just thought maybe . . ."

"Yes?"

"Really I'm just checking in. Things okay up there?"

"Fine, Al, fine."

"Checking in, and thanking you again for the trip. This is quite a place."

"You like it?"

"Love it. Thanks again."

"You're welcome, Al. You earned it," Kleiman said, and Al could picture him kindly smiling, the thin mustache stretched into gray rays across his lip. "Enjoy and get home safe. We miss you here."

Al almost said he missed them too, but then was stopped by the galling and ridiculous sensation that if he said it he would start to cry.

Instead he said, "Hey, I'll be back soon. You'll see, I'll be tan and sell my ass off. Better than before."

17

"*So what now?*" asked Chop Parilla.

"I wish you'd quit askin' me that," said Squid. "Every time I'm baskin' inna glow of something, you're already buggin' me what's next."

They were sitting at a beachfront restaurant at the south end of Duval Street. It was a seafood joint but they were having burgers; ever since the calamari they hadn't felt like fish. Chop looked off at the ocean. The last light was skimming across it, making it look both thick and glassy, like if soup could be a mirror.

"Somethin's up my ass about this job," he finally admitted.

"Yeah," said Squid. "You only got to steal one car." He was eating french fries. He ate them one by one, the long way. He blobbed the tips in ketchup then held them up above his mouth like a trainer dangling herrings to a seal.

"Nah," Chop said, "it isn't that. It's . . . it's . . . ah the hell with it."

Squid wiped ketchup from his lips. He found it entertaining when Chop tried to explain himself. "Come on," he urged. "What?"

Chop took a bite of burger, slowly chewed. "It's that . . . it's that ya got no waya knowin' when you're finished, when ya've done the job. Ya see what I'm sayin'?"

Squid sucked his Coca-Cola through a straw.

"I mean," said Chop, "ya torch a place, the place burns down, ya've done the job. Ya hurt a guy, he's inna hospital, ya've done the job. But this? Ya bother 'im, ya bother 'im some more—how ya know when ya've bothered 'im enough and the job is really done?"

Squid folded his hands and serenely smiled, confirmed in his most basic belief—a belief that allowed him to feel his efforts did not go totally unappreciated. He'd always held that an intrinsic sense of art, however rudimentary and inarticulate, existed even in the densest dullard. "So you're saying it's about the structure of the thing?"

"Fuck structure. What I'm sayin'—"

"Is that you want a rise and fall, a climax."

"What I want," said Chop, "is to know when the fuckin' job is over so I can go home to Hialeah and play wit' motors."

Squid went back to eating french fries. "S'okay," he said, "in your own mind, what would it take for the job to be over?"

"Fuck difference does it make?"

"Come on," said Squid. "We're talkin' hypothetical."

"Fuck hypothetical. Lemme eat my burger."

Berman sighed. "Chop, ya know what separates us from monkeys? We converse while dining, we make witty conversation. So come on. What would convince you that we did enough, the job is over?"

Parilla put his burger down. "Okay. Okay. The fucker's hauled off in a straitjacket. Or better yet, he dies."

Squid clasped his hands together, looked up at the deepening violet sky. "Beautiful! Perfect classic endings. Except that ain't the job."

"I kinda wish it was. Now lemme eat my fucking dinner."

He'd had one forkful of coleslaw when Squid was at him again.

"What this job is," the bandy man said, "the beauty of it, it's modern."

"Fuck modern."

"It doesn't finish. It's just there. Like one a those paintings that's just dribs and drabs and slashes all the way to the edge. Forces you to deal with tension."

Chop put down his fork. "Keep talking and you're gonna deal with my foot up your ass."

"Ya see the power of that tension? I mean, it even gets to you!"

"One more word, Squid. One more word."

The bandy man swallowed viscously and finally shut up. Eating french fries, he stared off at the ocean, which had given up its copper tinge and turned a nighttime indigo. With neither rise nor fall, it spread to the horizon, and was everywhere a climax, since it had no start or finish. The most ancient and most modern picture. He wished he could make Chop see it. He knew he never would.

Big Al Marracotta, an all-or-nothing guy, could not accept that his vacation had been tarnished, that his carefree, sex-dazed time in Florida should be anything less than perfect. It offended him that problems dared intrude; it frustrated him that he could not shut off the world; it made him bitter that pleasure wasn't simple.

So his attitude got lousy and he did everything he could to make things worse. The change was very sudden, and understandably baffling to Katy Sansone.

Things had been going pretty well. She'd been giving him a back rub. They'd been talking about things, he'd been almost revealing. She'd felt like she was helping him, that they were getting close, almost like a real couple. Then the phone rang and she was banished to the bath.

Now, three quarters of an hour later, she was out of the tub, swathed in a robe, a towel turban on her head, and everything was different. Al looked mad again. "Things okay?" she innocently asked, shaking water from her ear.

He didn't answer and didn't look at her. He wasn't pacing anymore, just sort of wandering around the room.

Trying to be helpful, she said, "That phone call—?"

"There wasn't any phone call," he cut her off. "Remember that." He kept wandering, seeming to look for places where his small feet hadn't yet flattened the carpet.

"Al, is there anything I can do?"

There wasn't, and he held it against her that there wasn't. He stared at her from under his eyebrows, and in the stare was an unreachableness that was not very different from hate.

Katy still imagined that she must have done something to deserve that look. "If you're mad about how long I stayed at the beach—"

"I don't give a shit how long you stayed."

He went to the phone and ordered a bottle of scotch. Katy rubbed the towel against her scalp.

"Why don't you put an outfit on," he said.

At first she was happy he said it. Sex opened him up, if anything did. She scanned his face for some hint of the boy-devil grin, the wry, untempered zest that welcomed her into his selfishness awhile. But he didn't look zestful, just craggy and mean. She got worried in her stomach. She tried to sound playful. "Which one would you suggest?"

"Black."

She got some things from her suitcase and went back to the bathroom.

The liquor arrived while she was in there. Al poured himself a tumblerful and picked out a porno film. He pulled down the window shades; the last, dusky light put a lavender gleam around their edges, then faded, squandered, into night.

Katy emerged, walking stiffly on spike heels.

She wore a bra that lifted her breasts but didn't cover them, and panties that cinched her waist and thighs but left her sex exposed, made a lewd frame around a picture rendered vivid and obscene by lack of context. With effort she approached the bed.

She didn't mind being looked at; usually she enjoyed it. There was a kind of power in what she had to show. But now it didn't feel right.

It would not have taken much to put her at ease—a compliment or even just a smile would have sufficed. But Big Al couldn't manage it. He seemed aroused yet annoyed that she was there. Dressed but for his shoes, he leaned back on a stack of pillows and gestured for her to join him in the bed. Then, without a word or a touch, he used the remote to start the movie.

In the film, a man with muscles and a pointy beard was teaching a woman to submit. Leather straps bit into flesh. Wrists stretched in metal rings. Buttocks were pinkened as slaps combined with whimpers on the soundtrack. Cruel things were done to nipples.

Above the tinkle of chain and the crescendo of moans as pain imitated pleasure, Katy said, "I don't like this, Al."

He watched the film. He didn't answer.

"Come on," she said, "let's watch something else."

Al made no reply.

On the screen the woman's hair was being pulled, her loins assaulted with a device that looked medieval. Katy wondered if Al would notice if she closed her eyes. She didn't want to watch but she didn't want to make him angry. She narrowed her lids just far enough to make everything a blur, and amid the sounds of cursing and slapping, she watched a movie of her own. She saw the beach, a bright horizon flecked with distant sails. Green wavelets topped by tiny curls, silver foam sizzling and disappearing through a sieve of cool coarse sand.

When the film was over, Big Al took off his clothes and climbed on top of her. He wasn't kind; he wasn't unkind. He just started, then he moved awhile, and then he finished.

Katy Sansone surprised herself by feeling nothing. Nothing bad, nothing good. Still, the nothing that she felt had content. It was made of shame and frustrated caring and a tardy anger that was finally starting to ripen.

When he was done with her and had rolled aside, she walked slowly to the bathroom to wash. She faced herself in the mirror, regarded herself with curiosity but no expression. She realized after a moment that what she was looking for was something to be proud of. She studied her own eyes, she firmed her jaw. Then she took off the things that Al had bought her, the cupless bra and the panties that put her on display, and dropped them in the trash.

18

Alan Tuschman didn't leave his room that evening.

He was wrung out, his chest hurt, and he was half afraid that if he showed himself, yet another ludicrous and dreadful thing was bound to happen. His confidence was badly shaken, and in some primitive, unreasoning way, his feelings were hurt, as if he'd been cast out by all the world, turned into a pariah. He felt like he'd forgotten how to get along with people, how to do the simple things that got a person through the day. Like a voodoo curse, his run of bad luck spooked him, and thereby brought on more bad luck.

He took a shower, scraped his belly on a splinter that had somehow become embedded in his bar of soap. He ordered in a pizza, burned his mouth on cheese. He cut up a slice for the dog, and the two of them ate in mopey silence beneath the picture of the greenish women with the greenish breasts. Then they crawled, defeated, into bed. Al watched the slow and mollifying rotation of the ceiling fan, and let his mind go numb. . . .

But there's no medicine like sleep, and in the morning everything looked cheerier.

The salesman blinked through his window, saw giant philodendron leaves, pendant coconuts turning yellow, soft mist rising from the hot tub. Perspective returned. Pariah? Come on—he was a well-liked, friendly guy who'd had a few bad breaks. His luck would turn; he knew it. He was on a mission to

be happy—Jesus Christ, he thought, when did I really start believing that?—and one way or another he was going to pull it off.

Exercise, he decided. In sweat was sanity and peace. Always
had been; always would be. He'd take a good long run.

He pulled on a jock; there was youth and vigor in the feel of
the straps against his butt. He almost touched his toes a couple
times, then put Fifi on her leash and headed out the door, past
the topless woman doing yoga on a towel, past the European
threesome already giggling over thimble muffins, past the desk
clerk, dozing with his hand around a mug of coffee.

He ran up Elizabeth Street, crossed the road that had brought
him into town. He tried to think of his grimace as a smile, tried
not to notice that none of this was easy anymore. His knees and
spine didn't cushion his brain the way they used to. His eyeballs
bounced. He sucked air past the lingering tickle in his lungs,
past the weight of last night's pizza, and kept on going.

He reached the county beach, traced out its zigzag path, then
headed north along a row of condos. Fifi's paws made a pleasant
ticking on the pavement, and, for a while, it hurt less as he went.
He remembered what it was to win, to break into the open with
a football spinning toward him and the goal line chalked on matted grass. The sun got higher and seared his hairline. Without
breaking stride he pulled off his shirt.

At the beginning of the long promenade that led on to the airport and the houseboats, he began to feel that he should turn
around. His temples throbbed; there was a squish in his sneak-
ers that might have been blood from his blistered feet. But his
course was just reaching its most beautiful, with the green water
of the Straits stretching away toward Cuba, and emerald-tinged
clouds stalled above the Gulf Stream.

So, mouth parched and ankles clicking, he pressed on. Young
women passed him effortlessly on Rollerblades. Old hippies
scudded by on junky bikes whose fat tires hummed against the
concrete. He plodded along and his thoughts whooshed by like
distant traffic. Sex. Archaic ball games. Sales pitches finding

their apotheosis in commissions. Mostly he just wanted to keep on moving. Beyond worries, explanations. Past the need to figure stuff out. Onward to the time when this eerie and unsettling vacation would be over and he could ease himself again into the womb of the familiar.

It wasn't that Big Al Marracotta didn't know he'd been a prick. He knew; but he'd started on a downward spiral and he just couldn't turn the thing around.

Over breakfast in their room, he watched Katy sulk, and he dimly understood that something different had come into her sulking. It was no longer a ploy. She wasn't doing it for attention or to get her way. She was doing it because she felt lousy and wanted to be left alone. She sat there with her bathrobe pulled in tight across her collarbones. She hadn't bothered to smooth her spiky hair, and her gaze floated without focus toward the curtained window.

Big Al looked down and stabbed his eggs. He knew the situation could still be rescued. He could apologize, and she would understand. But there's no way he would do it. An apology conferred status, gave a certain power to the person receiving it. He wasn't starting down that road. What about the next time he acted like a scumbag—would she throw it in his face? Would he have to apologize again? Till respect was whittled away to nothing? No way . . . Not that he absolutely had to apologize. Not in so many words. He could probably get things back on track and still stop short of that, just sort of slide around it. Tell her he had a lot on his mind; she'd fill in the rest. . . . But why give her that much information, that much satisfaction? Start confiding in someone, and they started feeling close, and that bred expectations, and that made the whole thing a big pain in the ass.

The little mobster gnawed at buttered toast and realized he was getting mad at Katy. Last night he'd been a bastard; he had to justify it somehow, so today he was digging in his heels. He slurped coffee and turned a hard eye on her. He decided she wasn't that pretty. Her eyes were undramatic and when she pouted her mouth looked sharp. She was moody, sometimes she was luke-warm in the sack, and when vacation was over he'd probably break up with her. Enough already. Be a sport, pay a couple months' rent on the studio in Murray Hill, and have it over with.

Thinking that, he felt restless in advance. He pushed his plate away, said, "Come on, let's take a drive or somethin'."

"Fine," said Katy, even more eager than he to be out of that hotel room.

As if it were her fault, he added, "I mean, Christ, we been here days and haven't seen a thing."

She almost answered that, then realized there was no point. Silently, she blotted her mouth on her napkin and moved off someplace private to get dressed.

19

Carlo Ganucci was surprised how readily Tony Eggs had agreed to sit down with Nicky Scotto. He thought he'd say a flat-out no, or at least demand to be persuaded.

Sitdowns were a nuisance. It was always someone bitching, and in the end you didn't give them what they wanted, and they went away madder than they were before; or you granted what they asked for, which almost always meant that someone else got mad and started looking for a meet.

So when, the evening before, the *consigliere* had passed along Nicky's request to get together, he'd done so in the offhand manner of a man expecting a terse and bothered refusal. But Tony Eggs had not seemed bothered. In fact he'd almost smiled. Dry lips twitched briefly back from yellow and insecurely rooted teeth, and his eyes took on a gratified gleam. "Good," he'd said.

"Good?"

"Good. Tell 'im ten tomorrow morning."

Now it was the appointed time, and Nicky Scotto, plucking at his cashmere turtleneck and smoothing the lapels of his slate-blue mohair suit, had just walked into the social club on Prince Street.

He was trying to look casual and confident. He waved to a couple of goombahs playing poker in a corner, kidded with the lackey behind the coffee counter. But when his espresso was handed to him, he couldn't quite keep the cup from chattering against the saucer. He squeezed it hard to hold it still, before moving to the inviolable table at the rear, where the two old men were sitting.

He waited for a nod from Tony Eggs, then almost daintily hitched up his trousers and joined them. Raising his demitasse, he said, "Tony. Carlo. Thank you for your time. *Salud.*"

He swallowed some coffee, struggled to put the cup down cleanly. A silent second passed, and he quickly understood that no one was going to help him keep the conversation going. Carlo Ganucci looked sleepy and feeble, the thin skin sallow and papery around his eyes. Tony Eggs appeared as inclined toward chitchat as a tree. Nicky cleared his throat, made a theatrical gesture of blowing into his hands, and said, "Fuckin' freezin' for November, huh?"

Neither old man answered that. Tony Eggs pulled his tongue down from the roof of his mouth. It made a clicking sound that seemed very loud.

Nicky tried again. "Okay, why I'm here, the reason, it's about the market."

Nobody responded. Carlo looked down at his crumbling yellow fingernails.

"I'm really happy to be runnin' it again," said Nicky. "Wanted to thank you for the opportunity."

"Who said it's an opportunity?" Tony Eggs Salento rumbled forth at last.

This flustered Nicky. He reached for his espresso cup, put it down again, tried a couple times to get a sentence started. Outside, horns honked and cabbies cursed each other.

Tony Eggs, suddenly loquacious, went on. "Hey, Nicky, how much that suit cost?"

"Eighteen hundred." He tried to keep the pride out of his voice, almost managed. He loved that suit. It wasn't just the money he'd been able to pay for it. It was that the guy who made it was in great demand, and wouldn't tailor clothing for just any-body.

The old boss pursed his lips. His own suit cost two-fifty off a downtown rack, and he'd had it twenty years. "Do me a favor," he told his young lieutenant. "Take the jacket off and stomp it."

"Excuse me?"

"If you'd like this meeting to continue, put the jacket onna goddamn floor and walk all over it."

Nicky licked his lips, glanced from underneath his brows at one old man and then the other. Maybe this was some kind of a test, or better yet a joke. But he saw no whimsy in their eyes. He waited an instant longer for a reprieve that would not come, then stood up, hesitated, and finally slipped out of his jacket and dropped it to the floor. For a moment he regarded it with heart-break and nostalgia, as though it were a dying pet. The old linoleum was dusty and cracked, with tarry fissures that would claw at a gray silk lining. And who could say what unspeakable residue of fish slime or dogshit might be clinging to his shoes?

His legs trying their damnedest to hold him back, he side-stepped onto the swath of custom-tailored mohair. He made a weak, little grinding motion then stepped off again.

"More," said Tony Eggs.

"More?"

Gingerly he stepped again onto his jacket; then, with a per-verse and mounting energy, a cresting wave of debasement and inchoate rage, he stomped the precious garment. He marched on it, he ran in place; he improvised a cha-cha, launched into a sort of demented Mashed Potato. His chest grew warm, his face flushed. He ground his heel into a sleeve, heard a seam rip open under the unsprung fury of his war dance. A drop of sweat broke free from a sideburn and trickled down his cheek, and he kept jumping on his jacket for several seconds after Tony said to him, "Okay, Nicky. Now siddown."

He sat. He was breathing heavily. He looked down at his ravaged jacket, and he almost wanted to cry. Cry, or tear it thread from thread, till no two pieces of it hung together, till it was as utterly destroyed as though it had never been made.

Softly, relentlessly, Tony Eggs Salento said, "Enough fun and games. Now we talk. . . . I know why you came here, Nicky. You came here 'cause you want the market back. But here's the problem: How can you expect to get it back when you still don't understand why you lost it inna first place?"

Nicky looked down at his hands, very pink against the green felt of the table. Carlo Ganucci gave a weak and sudden burp, the burp of a man whose innards weren't working right.

"Why'd ya lose the market, Nicky?" Tony Eggs went on. "Not because ya didn't run it good. Because ya got above yourself. *Capice?*"

Nicky tried to lift his eyes, but couldn't. His jaw worked and he felt it deep inside his ears.

"Ya got to where ya thought that Nicky Scotto was more important than the job. The suits, the nightclubs—they gave you a hard-on, they got you laid. Fine. But, Nicky, listena me. I'm sevenny years old and I ain't been inna can in forty-five years. Why? 'Cause I wear cheap suits and I stay home at night, and I don't rub the feds' faces inna shit I'm gettin' away with. Ya see?"

The lieutenant raised his face at last. Around his mouth and eyes, defiance and humiliation were contending, as on the face of every child who's been scolded.

"So, very simple," Tony Eggs resumed, "here is why you lost the market. You lost the market because you acted like a dumb trash show-off punk who was bound to fuck up big time and get himself nailed. . . . Now, have I made you feel like a piece a shit?"

There was no answer to that, so Nicky Scotto just looked around the room. Had the poker players heard all this, the lackey behind the counter?

"'Cause here's the funny part," said Tony Eggs. "I like you, Nicky. You're hungry. Ya work hard. Ya got potential. So now I'm in, like, a difficult position."

Nicky moved his lips. Getting his voice to work again was like starting up a long-parked car whose battery had run down. "What's difficult about it?" he managed.

The boss pulled on his long thin face. "I think you've learned a lesson. All things bein' equal, you deserve a second chance. But inna meantime, Big Al's got the market, and up until a couple days ago I was very happy wit' the job he was doin'."

Hope scratched at Nicky like loose threads in his underwear. He looked down at his violated jacket, felt a sudden spartan contempt for it. Who needed fancy suits? "And now?" he said.

Tony Eggs scratched his neck. He leaned his head forward to do so, and his throat went stringy in his collar. "Al made a couple judgments that sorta shook my confidence. Took vacation. Picked the wrong guy ta leave in charge while he was gone. It's not enough to fire him about. But—"

"But what?" said Nicky.

Tony Eggs leaned far back in his chair. So did Carlo Ganucci. The two old men took deep, sighing breaths, then, in unison, leaned forward once again.

"Nicky," said the boss, "I'm a pretty simple guy. I've always believed that the best man for the job is the man who wants the job the most."

Scotto pressed his ribs against the table, grabbed the edges of it with his meaty hands. "So what can I do—?"

Tony Eggs cut him off with a shrug. "I'm not you, Nicky. I don't know what you should do. Think about it. You'll come up wit' somethin'."

The boss looked away, and Nicky felt suddenly drained, belatedly realized that the old man's unblinking stare had been on him for a long, long time. He brought his hands in front of him, sat through a few seconds of silence before he understood that the sitdown was over. Without another word he rose to go. The rubber cups on his chair legs made ugly squeaks against the old linoleum.

"Your jacket," Tony Eggs reminded him as he started moving toward the door.

Nicky left it lying where it was.

"Cold outside," said Carlo Ganucci.

Nicky didn't turn around. With only his thin cashmere sweater for protection, he broke out into the unseasonable chill of the November morning, his mind already chewing on the question of what he had to do to get the market back.

20

Alan Tuschman, fleeing everything and nothing, ran farther than he should have.

He ran till his saliva was all used up, till he could feel the separate, grinding pieces that comprised his knees, till small fillets of muscle began to quiver in his buttocks. By now he was way up near the airport. Absently he watched planes take off and land, thought about the passengers briefly trading one life for another, carrying in their luggage the people they might be if nobody they knew was watching. The sun grew higher, shadows seemed to evaporate on hot pavements. The breeze dropped and the ocean took on the fuzzy sheen of brushed aluminum. Fifi's tongue hung down almost to the sidewalk, swung like a damp pink pendulum as she unflaggingly ran.

Just beyond the airport, the island curved, and there was a wide place in the promenade where people sometimes parked their cars, to fish, or windsurf, or just to look out at the Straits. Nearing that curve, sweat in his eyes and fog in his brain, Al saw something that at first glance made him smile. It was a new gray Lincoln, spotless but for the inevitable goo of squashed bugs on the windshield, and it had a New York license plate that said BIG AL.

Hmm, thought Alan Tuschman. Small world.

In the next heartbeat, though, something darker and indefinably discomfitting pressed in on him. He felt somehow crowded in his own skin. As if the basic fact of his uniqueness were being questioned. As though the borders of the little space he took up in the world were being suddenly contested.

He didn't have long to think about it. After half a dozen more strides, he saw the tall woman he'd spoken with on the way to the beach. She was sitting on the seawall, wearing pink shorts and a lime-green top, looking out across the ocean. The big, drooling rottweiler that he'd first seen on Duval Street was lolling around her ankles.

Al stopped running. He didn't exactly decide to stop. He just pulled up short, sucked in a breath, and yelled out, "Hi there!"

The woman turned toward his voice. It seemed to Al that she started to smile then caught herself. Her eyes flicked toward the Lincoln then back again. Blandly, uncomfortably, she said, "Oh, hi."

Fifi ran over and started yipping at the rottweiler, crouching on her chicken-wing back legs and sticking out her flat and tiny face. Ripper quailed, retreated behind Katy's slender calves.

Al Tuschman, proud of his dog, said, "Don't worry. She won't hurt him."

Katy almost smiled before erasing it again, gave Fifi a quick pat on the head. Her face tightened and her hand pulled back as the Lincoln's driver's-side door clicked open.

Al Marracotta got out. He hadn't previously seen the point of getting out to look at water that you could see just as easy through the windshield, but now he did. He was on the far side of the car, and could barely peek over its roof. He secretly came up on tiptoe to appraise this sweating palooka who was talking to his girlfriend. The guy looked strong. Moisture glistened in his whorls of thick black chest hair, veins stood out in his neck and arms. But strong was strong, and tough was tough, and Al Marracotta had long ago learned that the two generally had squat to do with each other. He snarled at the interloper and turned to Katy. "You know this guy?"

"We met at the beach." She sounded weary, maybe frightened, saying it.

"Two minutes you're outa my sight, you're pickin' up guys at the beach?"

Katy said nothing, looked down at the tangle of dogs at her feet.

Al Tuschman, trying to be helpful, agreeable, said, "Hey, we said hello. We hardly talked." Then he gestured toward the Lincoln's stern. "You know, my nickname's Big Al too."

Al Marracotta didn't like that. He was not a man inclined to share. Not girlfriends, not nicknames, not anything. He pushed forward his chin and said, "What of it?"

Disarmed by the readiness of the other man's hostility, Al Tuschman gave an awkward and retreating laugh. "Nothing. Just a funny coincidence, that's all."

Al Marracotta sneered and looked away. "Real fuckin' funny." To Katy, he said, "Come on, flirt, we're outa here."

She took a deep breath then rose from the seawall. She didn't look at Alan Tuschman, but he noticed once again how gracefully her long body folded and unfolded. Still, once she'd risen, there was a stiffness and a hesitation in her step, and anyone could see that she didn't want to get into that car. The cowardly rottweiler stayed behind her legs the whole way to the door, its veiny testicles bouncing as it leaped into the backseat.

Big Al Marracotta burned rubber as he pulled away. Big Al Tuschman sat down to rest where Katy had been sitting, used his balled-up shirt to dry his chest, and tried not to think about the long, stiff-jointed walk back to his hotel.

"*Come on,* Donnie, what else could he of meant?"

They were sitting in the fish market office. It was cold and it smelled of clamshells and the blue tang of slowly melting ice. Donnie Falcone kept his big funereal topcoat on; its lapels flapped as he gestured. "Coulda meant a lotta things," he said. "Up the take. Expand the territory. Increase the tribute. Ya know, do somethin' t'impress 'im. He didn't tell ya start a war."

Nicky Scotto drummed his fingers on his metal desk. Ambition was keeping him warm; he was still wearing the cashmere turtleneck alone. "What war?" he said. "I'm talkin' 'bout takin' out one guy."

"Lunatic!" said Donnie, pulling on his long and pliant face. "Listen ta yourself! You ain't takin' out nobody. Fuhget about it."

Nicky leaned back in his chair. It was a crappy chair, the cheap springs creaked as he leaned back, but, boy, did it feel comfortable. His face went dreamy, piggy black eyes losing focus.

Donnie leaned far across the scratched-up desk, grabbing for his friend's attention like he was reaching for a grip on someone halfway out a window. "Nicky, listena me. This wanting the market back. It's like a whaddyacallit, an obsession already. It's makin' you crazy."

"Crazy?" Nicky said placidly. "No. It's business, Donnie. Tony needs ta see how much I want the job. This is what he said."

Donnie closed his eyes a second, seemed to be praying for more patience. It didn't come. He sprang up from his chair, did a pirouette on the scuffed and damp floor, and pointed an accusing finger at his friend. "Goddamit! This is what I tol' you from the start!"

"*What* is what you tol' me from the start?"

"This crazy bullshit wit' the clams, the puking. It was never about that. Right from the start you were lookin' for a way to get the market back."

Nicky Scotto didn't bother to deny it. He folded his hands and smiled. He looked around the office. Minute by minute it was feeling more like his again. Pretty soon he could throw away the pictures of Big Al's wife and kids. Throw them in a Dumpster with the fish guts and the slime.

"For the love a Christ," his friend implored, "don't go any further wit' this, Nicky. The man has friends. Allies. You don't know the shit you're steppin' into."

Nicky Scotto pursed his lips, cocked an ear toward the shouts and laughs that now and then filtered in from the market, sounds full of vigor and comradeship and profit.

Then he said, "Hey, Donnie, ya know where I can get some cheap but decent suits? Right off the rack like?"

21

When the call came from New York, Squid Berman was at the aquarium, doing research.

He studied up on barracuda, with their steam-shovel jaws and beveled pins for teeth; on manta rays, whose three-foot tails were barbed like those of ancient devils; on giant octopi, whose suction-cup legs could reduce a man to a polka-dotted cushion of suppurating hickeys. He spent an entertaining hour and took away a couple good ideas.

He got back to the motel to find Chop all excited, rubbing the top of his head and not stopping till his hand had stroked his stump of neck and was reaching toward his shoulders.

"Talked ta Nicky," the car specialist reported.

"Didja tell 'im about the lobsters?" Berman asked with pride. "Didja tell 'im about—?"

"He wants ta change the job."

"Change the job? But I just been thinking—"

"He wants we clip the guy."

Squid's face fell and he sat down on the bed. His bony hands fretted in his narrow lap and his knees would not stay still. "Clip the guy? Ah fuck. I don't wanna clip the guy."

Chop was pacing the length of the dresser. His face was changing too, getting into character for the new assignment. Skin tightened at the edges of his eyes, his lips flattened out and pulled in against his teeth. "Squid," he said, "don't tell me you're goin' tenderhearted on me."

"It isn't that," said Berman. "Guy dies, doesn't die, who gives a shit? It's just that . . ." His tongue probed around inside his cheeks, he gave a series of spasmodic little shrugs.

"Just what?"

Squid threw his hands up in the air. "Just that this has been, like, a really one-of-a-kind job so far, and now the motherfucker's makin' it bourgeois."

"Boozh-wah?"

"Ya know. Ordinary. Obvious. I hate that shit."

Chop said, "We get an extra fifty grand. It's gonna be a piece a cake."

Disgusted, Squid turned his back, looked at a dead fly snagged and hollowed out in a spiderweb at a corner of the room.

Chop continued anyway. Without seeming to notice he was doing it, he tugged at his wrist like he was pulling on a glove. "We grab the piece a shit outside his hotel. Take 'im up the Keys, ice 'im, dump 'im inna mangroves. Boom, it's over. T'ree hours later we're home, checkin' out titties on South Beach. Beautiful."

Petulantly, still looking away, Squid said, "I'm not doin' it."

Chop pivoted around the bed, wedged his way into the other man's field of vision. "Whaddya mean, you're not doin' it? Come on, now, don't embarrass me. I tol' Nicky no problem, we'd do it."

Berman sulked and salivated. He swallowed hard, his hands fluttered like contending birds. He shook his head.

Chop Parilla pawed the carpet, breathed hard through his mouth. In desperation he said, "I never knew Sid Berman to go half-ass on a job."

This got to Squid, hit him where he lived. He blinked, he squirmed, he moved his tongue to a mouth corner and left it there awhile. Finally he said, "Okay, okay, we'll take him out. On one condition."

Chop's eyes rolled up toward his low and deeply furrowed forehead. "What's the condition?"

Squid gave a determined sideways tilt to his head. "We finish the job the way we started it."

"And fuck is that supposed to mean?"

"We take 'im out by seafood."

Chop roughly spanked his thighs as he sprang out of his crouch. "Fuckin' seafood? Squid, Jesus Christ! Why ya gotta make everything so difficult?"

Calmer now, more settled in his mind, Squid folded his bandy arms across his chest. It wasn't about difficulty. It was about unity, integrity. Did you begin a statue with a hammer and chisel and suddenly switch to a chain saw? No, you were true to the tools you started with. That was a basic rule of craft. Fundamental.

Chop hadn't dropped his protest. Fists balled, knees bent in a simian slouch, he was working off frustration in great bounds around the narrow, mildewed room. "Ya take guys out wit' guns," he said. "Ya take guys out wit' knives. Baseball bats. Piana wire. What kinda horseshit is ya take a guy out wit' seafood?"

Knowing that he'd won, Squid spoke very softly. "Death by seafood, Chop," he said. "Either that, or you get yourself a different partner."

Alan Tuschman leaned forward at his tiny table at an outdoor restaurant that overlooked the harbor, and bit deep and lustily into his grouper sandwich.

The thin crust of the Cuban roll caved in beneath the clamping of his teeth; mayo squished against his gums; the crunch of onion lit a small fire on his tongue; and the fish's charbroiled surface blended the tastes of ocean and woods. He savored the bite a good long moment, then washed it down with beer.

He couldn't remember when he'd tasted food so vividly, and vaguely wondered why it seemed so new and marvelous. Perhaps his recent sufferings, coupled with the humid vacancy of his days, made him more appreciative of simple things, the mundane pleasures too often shouted down by busyness, routine. Maybe it was just that his long run had quieted his mind and opened up his body, lulled him back to basics.

In any case, he thoroughly enjoyed his lunch and was in calmly buoyant spirits as, led by Fifi, he strolled back to his hotel. Everything was oddly perfect on that stroll. A brilliant sun warmed him, but seemed to duck behind a scrap of cloud whenever he grew too hot. Locals with groceries in their bike baskets smiled at him as if he'd suddenly come to belong. Papery bougainvillea petals came unstuck in soft breezes and fluttered down russet and fuchsia in his path, and he decided that today was the day he'd get naked at the pool.

He strolled through the gate of Paradise, and the desk clerk called to him.

Al's posture drooped, his euphoria imploded. By now it was Pavlovian. What next? The desk clerk had bad news only, and delivered it always with a smarmy and malicious smile. On legs suddenly grown heavy, Al walked into the office.

The clerk looked at him from between the ruby studs above his eyebrow and the purplish bags beneath his eyes. His mouth was sardonic, his tone as irritating as ever, but shockingly, his news today was good. "There's someone waiting for you at the pool," he said. "A woman."

Al took in the information as though his ears were in his pants. "A woman," he punchily echoed. "Waiting for me."

"You're the tall guy named Al."

"This is true." He swallowed. He knew who it was, of course. His near-lover, the woman with the wonderful thick hair. The woman whose unclothed torso he'd briefly held against his own. She'd come to realize he wasn't kinky after all, that the lobsters in the sheets were some grotesque but blameless accident. She'd returned in the sober light of day to finish what they'd started. It would be even sweeter for the long delay.

Alan Tuschman pulled down smartly on his shirtfront, wished he hadn't had the onion on his sandwich. He turned with almost military crispness and walked out toward the pool.

He scanned the helter-skelter ranks of lounges for that mass of springy hair, the fleshy shoulders and heavy breasts that he remembered.

Then he spotted Katy, the woman with the nasty boyfriend. She was laid out long and thin and ill at ease, save for Al the only person in the place with clothes on.

22

"Hi," she said as he sat down on a lounge beside her. She said it sheepishly, but packed into the single syllable, as well, was a suggestion of bent humor and a head-shaking acceptance of the fact that things seldom went as planned.

Al fumbled through a greeting in return.

"Surprised to see me," she said. It was not a question. She patted Fifi's knobby head. The dog licked her hand.

"How'd you know where—?"

"You told me," she reminded him. "On the road to the beach."

"Ah."

She glanced furtively around the courtyard at the European threesome, the fuzzy lesbians, the basted gay men with their bronzed and dimpled buns. "Kind of an amusing place."

"Kind of is," said Al. He had no idea why she was there, but could not help suspecting some sick game with himself as beard. His gaze wandered over to the courtyard gate. He half expected to see the sneering jealous boyfriend come barging through it, shaking his fists and sticking out his feisty chin and making an appalling scene.

Katy followed his eyes, understood his thoughts. The playfulness fell out of her voice, and suddenly she sounded very young and very lost. "I just walked out on him," she said. "I didn't know where else to go. I'm sorry."

Al looked at her more closely then. The sun was in his eyes, and it wasn't until he shaded them with his hand that he saw the red place on her jawbone, just below the ear.

She saw him looking at it, and was horrified and ashamed. She hadn't known there was a mark. Her composure let go and she cried for half a second. A tiny whimper escaped. A tear swelled at the corner of her eye, then vanished, as though by sheer act of will she could suck it back.

"Are you okay?" Al Tuschman asked her.

She nodded that she was, and looked away. It was all so stupid, she was thinking. So pointless. The second they'd sped off from the promenade, Big Al had started cursing at her, calling her names. She was a tramp, a slut, an ingrate. She'd crossed her arms and rolled her eyes and slunk against her door. He drove a little ways up the Keys, then stopped and had a couple drinks while she sipped lemonade. For a while he calmed down; then, as they were getting back to town he started in again. Ugly words, ugly accusations. Finally she stood up for herself. She'd done nothing wrong. All she'd done was talk to someone for three minutes, and if he couldn't handle that, then he was really pathetic.

That's when he hit her. They were stopped at a red light, heavy traffic. He yanked a hand off the steering wheel and slapped her. It was a weak and awkward smack. It didn't hurt, and what made it yet sadder was that even Katy could see that he was trying to hold himself back. But he hadn't managed; he'd hit her. She stared at him a second. He stared back with what might have been remorse. But it was too late. She got out of the Lincoln and on milky knees she stormed away. She'd heard horns honking but didn't look back.

Now, at poolside, she took a deep breath and started sitting up. "Look," she said, "we don't even know each other. I shouldn't be bothering you like this."

"Are you bothering me?" Al Tuschman said. Mainly he was asking himself. "Hey, I'm on vacation. I'm bored out of my mind. Let's talk."

She hovered halfway out of her lounge a moment, studied

Alan Tuschman's face. There was kindness, she felt, in the spacing of the features. Big eyes, wide apart. A full and candid mouth. Fleshy olive cheeks with here and there a small and unembarrassed crater. She liked his face, yet found herself searching for the things that she was more accustomed to—suspicion, guile, temper. When she couldn't find them, she grew briefly confused. Her practiced toughness let go a little bit, and her back eased down again onto the chaise. "Oh, God," she said. "This is a helluva vacation."

Al pursed his lips, folded his hands. "Look," he said, "maybe you'll give things a little while to calm down—"

"Then what?" she interrupted. "Go crawling back? Look, I'm done with him about twenty seconds before he's done with me. And he's the wrong guy anyway. It was a stupid thing to be involved in in the first place."

"Why?" asked Al.

She gave a mirthless laugh. "Too many reasons to go into. Why feel even worse?"

"Okay," he said. "So what'll you do?"

She twisted up her mouth and shrugged. "Get a flight back home, I guess."

"What about your things, your luggage?"

Her face went briefly sour as she thought about the thongs, the garters, the underwire bras Big Al had bought her. "There's nothing there I care about," she said.

"You have a ticket?"

Katy shook her head. "We drove. The car. Remember?"

At this Al gave a rueful snort. "I drove too. I had a car back then. Same license plate. Isn't that a pisser?"

"Same license plate?" said Katy.

"I mean, Jersey, not New York, but, yeah, same plate."

Katy's mouth stretched into a cockeyed smile. "Christ, I wish you had a different name."

Al had no response for that, so he said, "You really sure you wanna leave?"

She didn't answer quite as fast as she meant to. But she sighed and said, "Yeah, I'm going. I'll try to find a friend up in the city, see if she can wire down some money."

"Wire money?" said Al Tuschman. It seemed like such a quaint idea, he smiled.

Katy took offense, her eyes unblinking beneath the spiky hair. "Look," she said, "I'm twenty-nine. Sometimes I work as a waitress. Cocktails, mostly. Lately I made the idiot mistake of letting a rich boyfriend pay my way. I happen not to have a credit card. That shock you?"

Blindsided by her sudden vehemence, Al Tuschman leaned back a little way. Why was she daring him to look down on her? "Hey," he said, "I'm not judging you."

She dropped her eyes, her hands fidgeted on her tummy. "Ah, shit. I'm judging myself. Nothing to do with you. I'm sorry."

Al said, "Three minutes, that's like the fourteenth time you've apologized."

There was a silence broken only by the ceaseless tittering of the Europeans and the soft splash of a naked man stepping gingerly into the pool. After a moment Al heard himself say, "Listen, if it's really what you wanna do, I'll lend you the money for a ticket home."

Katy looked at him, still fidgeting. With wonderment and not without mistrust, she said, "Why? Why would you do that for me?"

Al blew a little air between his lips, softly rubbed his hands together. "Why?" he said, and for a moment he wasn't the least bit sure himself. Then he leaned down, and in a conspiratorial whisper he continued. "I'll tell you why. 'Cause you and me, we're the only people in this town who will admit that vacation's going lousy." He reached a hand across the narrow space between their lounges. "Come on. Let's see about getting you a flight."

Chop Parilla should have known better, but he still imagined that maybe he could talk Sid Berman into doing the job his way. Over a late lunch at a dim and dusty place called the Half Moon Tavern, he said, "Jesus, Squid, this job could get done so much faster wit', say, a thirty-eight."

"Right," said Berman, eating french fries the long way. "And the Sistine fuckin' Chapel coulda got done so much faster wit' a roller. Zere somethin' that you're drivin' at?"

"I'd like to get back home sometime," said Chop.

Squid Berman frowned. Such thinking was beneath him. You didn't think of home when you were on a job. You didn't think of anything except the job. That was concentration. That was purity.

Chop gnawed the paltry meat off a chicken wing. "Sistine Chapel? Zat in Little Havana?"

To avoid laughing in his partner's coarse, uncultured face, Berman looked away. As he did so, in one of those serendipitous opportunities that only the concentrated mind is quick enough to seize, something caught his eye.

It was a stuffed fish nailed onto the cheap, fake paneling of the wall. The fish's back was an electric blue, its belly a metallic silver. From its gorgeously arched spine protruded a large webbed fin as graceful as a Japanese fan; extending from the tapering head was a nose that stretched and stretched, Pinocchio-like, into a two-foot spike.

Transfixed, Squid stared at the creature a long moment, then gestured for the waiter. "That fish," he said. "Zat a . . . whaddyacallit?"

"Sailfish," said the waiter.

"It's beautiful," said Squid.

The waiter nodded in wistful agreement. He was a burly guy who liked to fish. He wished that he was fishing now. "People catch 'em just beyond the reef," he said. "Usually release 'em nowadays. People don't make real trophies anymore."

"How'd they used to do 'em?" asked Squid.

"The real ones? They'd peel back the skin, sever the back-bone, pop the eyes, scoop the brains out with a little pick—"

"Hey," said Chop, "I'm eatin' heah."

"Sorry," said the waiter. "The new ones, they're just paint and plastic over Styrofoam."

"But that one's real?" asked Squid. It was important to him that it was.

"Pretty sure," the waiter said. "Been there years and years."

Casually, Squid said, "How sharp's the nose?"

"You mean its sense of smell?"

"No. I mean, the nose, how sharp, ya know, for sticking things."

The waiter let out a respectful sound. "Like a razor. That's how he feeds. Gets into a school of jack or yellowtail and just starts slashing. Sometimes hacks 'em up, sometimes runs a fish right through."

Moisture was pooling beneath Squid's tongue. He swallowed hard, said to Chop, "Hey, Joe, wouldn't it be great to tell the folks back home we caught one a those?"

Parilla, still working on his plate of wings, his celery and blue cheese dressing, was slow on the uptake, didn't answer.

Squid said to the waiter, "How much ya want for it?"

The waiter gave a nervous laugh. "It isn't mine. It isn't for sale."

"Okay, okay, but how much is it worth?"

The waiter shrugged. "You see 'em now and then, antique stores, estate sales, three, four hundred."

"Take two thousand?"

The waiter paused to see if he was kidding.

"Cash. Right now," Sid Berman damply said. "Look, we gotta drive back t'Ohio right after lunch."

The waiter said, "You're serious. I'll ask the manager."

While he was gone, Chop said, "Two grand, Squid? You're fuckin' crazy."

Squid was looking at the seafood with the razor nose. "Worth every penny," he said. "The absolutely perfect ending don't come cheap."

They left with the stuffed fish tucked under Squid's proud arm like something he'd won at a carnival.

23

For Big Al Marracotta, things went from bad to worse. He'd reached that stage of being mad where he had no clue who he was really mad at.

Back in his hotel room, alone, he nipped into what was left of last night's scotch and decided that everyone was betraying him, everyone was letting him down. His goombahs up in the city. One asshole gets himself indicted. Does anybody think of telling Al, giving him some notice? No, he's gotta be put through the embarrassment, the humiliation, of having it thrown in his face by the bosses. And what do they do? Do they talk to him like a man, a respected colleague? No, they cut him right out of the loop, treat him like a punk who needs a lesson, and put his worst enemy in charge. Nicky Scotto. Preening wiseass conceited cocky shithead!

And why does all this happen? Why? Because he's trying to have a short vacation with a woman who turns out to be an ungrateful flirty bitch. Couple of hours on her own, she's throwing herself at some big hairy guy with muscles. And does she have one shred of sympathy or understanding for what he's up against, the pressure that he's under? Does she cut him any slack at all? No. He has one tiny second of losing his temper, and she has the gall to walk.

Well, she'd be back—he had no doubt of that. All her stuff was here; he was still her ticket home. She'd walk off her hurt feelings, size up her situation, and return.

But what if she returned and found Al moping and drinking in their empty room? How would it look? It would look like he was a little bit lost without her, like he had nothing better to do than brood and pace and wait to see if they could turn things around and maybe try again.

It wouldn't do to have her see that, think that. Wouldn't do at all.

So Big Al Marracotta, clutching his glass in one hand, started undressing with the other. He'd get into his cabana suit and go down to the pool. Let Katy know he wasn't about to piss away the day just because she got huffy. Let her see that he was perfectly content to tan alone, sneaking peeks at the breasts and asses of other men's girlfriends, sipping coladas at the swim-up bar without the hassle of a moody, flirty woman cluttering up his mind.

"Nothing till nine-thirty," said the desk clerk, muffling the phone against his chest. He said it with a smile, happy in the knowledge that it caused inconvenience to the suburban salesman and his unregistered, unpaid-for visitor.

"I'll take it," Katy said, bearing down to hold on to her resolve. Leaving was never easy, and leaving something awful was in some ways harder than leaving something almost good.

"So what now?" Al asked her, when the booking had been made. "Wanna hang out here?"

Secretly, the desk clerk winced. Ruby studs moved above his eyebrow.

Katy bit her lip, considered. "What I'd really like to do is go back to the beach. See that green water. Wanna come along?"

This sounded good to Al. After these few days wholly on his own, it was a relief to have someone else suggest a plan. But he could not help glancing down at his blistered feet. "How 'bout we call a cab."

Katy suddenly brightened. Her jaw relaxed, her eyes got wide, she stopped looking like somebody's mistress and resembled instead a kid with a day off from school. "Let's rent bikes!" she said. "That's what people do here. Rent bikes and ride around with maps."

Al cleared his throat to stall for time. He hadn't ridden a bicycle in many years.

Wanting to be rid of them so he could settle back into his semi-doze, the desk clerk said, "There are a couple here that you could use."

So they got on clunky one-speed cruisers and rode off to the beach.

Al put Fifi in his basket. She clamped her tiny claws around the wire mesh as her master jerked the handlebars, causing palms and mopeds and other bicyclists to sweep past in a sun-shot blur. Katy seemed unhindered by her high-heeled sandals; without apparent effort she stood up on the pedals and held her slender butt above the seat. They rode through the faux-Bahamian development and down the sandy road between the navy fences until they reached the shore.

Afternoon was well advanced by then. The Australian pines threw long and feathery shadows. Sunburned people with beach chairs held in the crooks of their arms were heading for the parking lot. On the water, catamarans were returning from the reef; the yellow sun seemed at moments to balance on their giant masts. Al and Katy sat down at a spot where the sloping sand was at an angle like a lounge.

Katy curled up, knees to chest, and stared out at the water as though she didn't expect to see anything so beautiful for a long, long time, as if trying to memorize the shifting patterns of emerald green with gold-white flashes. At some point she glanced at Alan Tuschman's striped Bermudas. "Jeez," she said, "I didn't even give you time to change. You could've swam."

"Not me," said Al. "Swam here yesterday. Got chased by a shark."

"A shark?"

"Were, like, thirty other people swimming. Thing zeroed in on me like it had radar."

Katy shook her head. "Car heist. Shark attack. Now you're stuck baby-sitting me. You always so unlucky?"

"You always so down on yourself?" he countered.

It was mostly just a reflex quip, but Katy took the question seriously. She'd kicked off her sandals; now she sighed and buried her toes in sand. "No," she said. "I don't think always. Just the last thirteen, fourteen years or so."

Al did not know what to say to that. He lay back on his hands, felt hot sun underneath his chin.

As if she were talking to herself, Katy said, "Before that I think I was a pretty happy kid. Felt safe. Felt confident. Then I sort of messed it up."

Alan Tuschman briefly weighed the words, then said, "Got pregnant?"

Katy swiveled toward him, sand making a crunching sound beneath her. "How'd you know?"

"I did the math and took a wild guess."

Katy stared down at her knees.

Al said, "Come on, everyone gets pregnant at that age."

"Not exactly everyone."

"Get pregnant, crash a car—everybody makes the same mistakes."

"Maybe," Katy said. "But not everybody's from a really Catholic family in a really Catholic neighborhood."

"Ah," said Al. "You had the kid?"

Katy nodded. "Dropped out of school. Hid out. A sinner with the nuns."

There was a pause. Offshore, a schooner tacked, its sails flapping like wet laundry until they filled.

Katy looked away and said, "I don't talk about this stuff."

"Hey, we're on vacation."

She didn't quite see what difference that made. "Your life is still your life."

"Okay. But you're allowed a little breather from it now and then."

Katy pouted. She watched Fifi busily digging a hole in the sand, wondered if the dog had some deep purpose in doing so. She surprised herself by going on. "You give away a baby, it's supposed to haunt you, right? Well, call me unmaternal, it isn't that for me. I mean, sure, it's weird to think I have a kid out there somewhere. But he, she—they're better off adopted. That's the simple truth. What gets me, though . . . I just lost my momentum. Never really got on track again. Forgot how to be a regular person around regular people. Understand?"

Al half nodded. He wanted to say something but nothing would come.

It didn't matter. Katy wasn't stopping now. "You know what it's like? It's like when people choose up sides in the playground. But now it's like the teams are the good people and the bad people. And once you make a big mistake, and your father calls you terrible things and your family is ashamed of you, you get put on the bad team. And then the people on the bad team are your friends, whether or not you really like them. They're your people. The good people—you sort of stop understanding them, stop knowing how to talk to them, stop knowing how to meet them even. So you're stuck. It doesn't change. You see?"

Al came up a little ways on sandy elbows. "Except it can change. Any day."

She tried to smile, waved her arms like she was swatting hope away. Again she looked off at the water. The colors kept changing as the sun slipped lower. Finally she said, "It's nice to talk to you." She twisted up her mouth. "I just wish you had a different name. Nickname, even. Didn't you ever have a different nickname?"

Al hesitated, then confessed. "Had one all through childhood. Hated it."

"What was it?"

He shook his head.

"Come on," she urged. "We're on vacation."

He reached forward, brushed some sand from above his dog's eyes. "Tusch."

"Tusch?"

"Last name's Tuschman. And as a kid I had a big behind."

"Tusch," she said again. "Mind if I call you that instead of, you know, that other name?"

Al grimaced though he didn't really mind.

"Come on," she said, "it's only for a few more hours."

He grabbed his dog and wrestled her a little bit. "Okay. What the hell," he said. "Only for a few more hours."

24

Big Al Marracotta was quietly flabbergasted when Katy had not returned by sunset. Very gradually, in blips of irritation and waves of masked regret, he lost his certainty that she was coming back at all.

He'd been drinking at a measured pace all afternoon, never quite getting drunk, but proceeding on a slow slide from anger and frustration to befuddlement and self-pity. At moments he even felt a grudging respect for his vanished girlfriend, for her moxie in standing up to him and skipping.

When thoughts like that began occurring to him, he'd wade over to the swim-up bar and have another cocktail.

The day dragged on. Eventually the sun dipped behind the building; an oblong of shadow crept across the pool. People started leaving. They left in couples; they had other things to do; and Big Al hated them for it. Curtains were drawn across the sliding glass doors of the lanai rooms. The shutters were closed on the towel kiosk. With maybe half a dozen sun-fried people still glued to their lounges, Big Al got up to leave. He was damned if he was going to be the last one there, lying by himself like some kind of loser.

He went back upstairs to the room. In spite of himself, pretending that he wasn't doing it, he snooped around to see if Katy had perhaps been by. Everything was as before. Her suitcase on its stand next to the armoire; her makeup kit on the bathroom counter, unzipped and gaping open. The two big bags of goodies from the porno store. They mocked him now: all those toys and no one to play with.

He sat down on the bed, reached deep for another dose of anger to chase away the gloom. "Fuck her," he said aloud, though with faltering conviction. He had three more lousy days down here before returning to the shitstorm in New York, and one way or another he was going to make them memorable.

He picked up the phone, called room service, and ordered himself a steak and a bottle of red wine.

Half an hour later, the waiter's knocking on the door woke him from a leaden sleep.

Katy and Al Tuschman watched sunset at the beach. They saw the sun squeeze out of round just before it touched the water; saw its reflection rise to meet it, transforming it for a time into a fat and melting candle; saw it slip at last beneath the surface like a vast quarter sliding down a slot.

Watching it together both was and was not wonderful. Sunsets were supposed to be romantic. You were supposed to watch them with your arm around someone. At the final instant, you kissed as a token of shared passage from bright day to tender evening, and then you strolled off in the twilight hand in hand.

Al and Katy, mere acquaintances in a nutty situation, did none of that. They sat with their knees and elbows close but not touching. As near as they came to contact was in taking turns petting the dog. They stared off at the sky until the sparse, underlit clouds had gone from flaming pink to a powdery lavender; then by silent agreement they stood, unceremoniously slapping sand off their bottoms. Al resisted looking at his watch. In the wistful awkwardness of the moment, he wasn't even sure if he wanted the time until Katy's departure to go faster or more slowly than was natural.

They walked to their bikes. Finally Al said, "Feel like a drink? Something t'eat?"

Katy, not used to being consulted, just shrugged at first, then said, "Sure."

They pedaled off between the navy fences, through the fake development; then, on Thomas Street, before they'd reached the busy part of town, they heard music coming from behind a wooden fence that was painted blue and pink and green. A hand-scrawled sign said the place was called Coco's. In place of valet parking, it offered a row of bike racks that were full of locals' clunkers.

"Chance it?" asked Al Tuschman.

Katy nodded, widened her eyes. They crammed their fat-tire bikes in among the others and went around the fence.

They walked through a short passageway and were immediately outdoors again—in a side yard paved in nothing but stomped earth. Well-spaced tables leaned in ruts, and no two tables matched. A hammock was strung between a rubber tree and a mahogany; an old man and a child seemed to be asleep in it. Chickens roamed around; Fifi sniffed their tracks. The music was Caribbean, took its slippery rhythms from the scratch and recoil of blowing palms, the surge and fizz of lapping waves.

Al and Katy moved to the far end of the place, found a vacant table with a rooster on it. Al shooed the bird away; it cackled out a protest, then half flew, half hopped, first to a chair back, then the ground.

"This is excellent," said Katy, sitting down.

Al was happy she was happy, pleased with himself for stumbling on a place she liked. He had to remind himself this was not a date.

The waitress came over and they ordered margaritas.

Clinking salty glasses, Katy gestured up toward swaying fronds against the jewel-box velvet of the sky, over at the dim bandstand where a Bahamian trio, cool beyond words, played like they could play forever, and said, "Cheers. Now *this* is what

I pictured. Now I feel like I'm on vacation." She sipped her drink and added, "Better late than never, huh?"

The comment made Al Tuschman unpleasantly aware of the watch on his wrist. "Hungry?"

She pursed her lips. "I could eat."

They ordered jerk chicken and popcorn shrimp.

Pretending to scratch a bug bite, Al sneaked a look at the time. It was ten of eight, and he too was only now beginning to feel like he was truly on vacation. Unless, that is, vacation truly felt like being lonely, and paranoid, and discombobulated.

"So Tusch," said Katy, "can I ask you something? Traveling alone—it's a fantasy of mine, I envy it. The freedom. You love it?"

Al pulled on an ear. "Has its moments," he said. "But the novelty's sort of over. I spend a lot of time alone."

She studied him, the strong shoulders and big kind face and curly hair. "How come?"

He shrugged. "I work a lot. Where I live, the 'burbs, it's sixteen-year-old girls in Camaros or soccer moms in minivans. I live long enough, I'll catch the next wave of divorcées."

"Ever married yourself?"

"Long time ago. Too young. Wrong person."

It was as good a time as any to signal for another round of drinks.

They clinked glasses once again, knocking loose damp salt. A breeze moved through the yard, carrying smells of spent flowers and clove and cinnamon from the kitchen. Katy took a small sip of her cocktail, then looked up and down and left and right, and said out of the blue, "Wanna dance?"

Al had still been thinking vaguely of his ill-considered past. The question took him by surprise. He pulled his brows together, let slip a nervous laugh, then glanced quickly, furtively around the yard. People were eating. People were drinking. Nobody was dancing. "I don't think this is a dancing place," he said.

"Come on," she said. "It's dirt. There's chickens. Who cares?"

"I don't know how to dance to this stuff."

But Katy was already getting up, her long body smoothly unfolding. "Please?" she said, holding out her hand. "I wanna be able to remember that I danced by moonlight in Key West. Come on—two minutes of your life."

With grave misgivings, Al Tuschman dabbed his big lips on his napkin, rose on creaky ankles.

Katy stood before him, ballroom style. He took her hand, which was very cool from cradling her drink. As lightly as he could, he held her waist. Warmth came through her shirt, he felt the long muscles that let her bend and rise so neatly. He silently counted several beats, then they started dancing. The dance they did was a little like a stiff-kneed samba, a little like the first fox-trot kids ever learn, sweaty-handed in the junior high school gym.

They'd danced for maybe thirty seconds, made it three quarters of the way around their small table, when the waitress showed up with their plates in either hand, trailing plumes of fragrant steam.

They dropped their hands and sat back down. A few people briefly applauded.

Al's face was flushed. His knees tingled and he was very aware of the pulse in his neck. None of this had to do with holding Katy in his arms; of that he was quite sure. She had a plane to catch in an hour and a quarter. She was the mistress of a jealous bully; she imagined she was finished with him, but chances are they would drift unwholesomely together once again. Besides, she wasn't even Al Tuschman's type—that spiky hair, the suspect lashes matted with mascara. No—this accidental excitement he was feeling . . . okay, this thrill—it didn't have to do with her. All it was, was nerves from standing up to dance with people watching. Neither more nor less than that.

He sipped his margarita and looked across the table. Katy was smiling broadly above her plate of shrimp. Her eyes were bright, and sinews stood out in her throat. "That was great," she said. "That was the nicest thing I've done down here. Thanks."

To his amazement and chagrin, Al heard himself say, "Wanna do it more?"

Katy had just picked up her fork. Now she was a little bit confused. She looked from Al to her shrimp and back again.

Himself confused, Al said, "I don't mean right this second." He seized his knife, cut into his chicken, and smiled weakly.

They had some bites of food.

"How's the time?" asked Katy. She said it as neutrally as it could be said, but still there was something like death in the words.

"Sucks," said Al. "How's the shrimp?"

"Umm," she said. Her mouth was full. She gestured for him to try some.

He did. He chewed awhile. Then he put his fork down. He looked at Katy, who was not his type and who, at the very least, was on an instant messy rebound. But they'd watched the sun go down together. They'd danced. He'd eaten off her plate. Knowing that he shouldn't say it, he said, "That plane. You really wanna go?"

She looked away and wiped her mouth. "Oh, Jesus. Please don't ask me that."

He sipped his drink. It had lost its chill and tasted very salty. The tireless musicians played without a lapse. He said, "Simple question. What's so terrible I'm asking?"

Katy said nothing. Her fork jabbed toward her shrimp again, and then it stopped midair.

Al found himself staring at her fingers. He could see that they were bearing down, blanched around the nails. He wondered if he was tipsier than he'd realized. Fumbling, he said, "Look . . . hey, listen . . . I don't know exactly how to say this. I'm not asking you to sleep with me."

Katy only gaped and blinked at that, touched, relieved, befuddled, and just a little bit insulted all at once.

143

"You wanna stay," he rambled, "we could see the town. Dance. There's a sofa in my room."

Katy dropped her fork, picked up her drink. "A sofa?" She looked past Al at the shrubbery, the arching palms, the orange mist around the streetlamps on this rare and humid night. Incredulous, she said, "You're asking me to be your roommate?"

25

Big Al and his rage woke up together from their nap.

Sitting on the edge of his vacant bed to eat his room-service steak, he thought angry thoughts that made him chew so hard he could feel it in the sockets of his teeth. An infuriating sense of wasted time assailed him. Time wasted on a moody broad who dragged him away from running his business and then turned out to be a flaky brat. Katy's betrayal—what else could he call it?—made him hanker to humiliate her, but it was tough to take revenge against someone who wasn't there. It called for ingenuity.

He ate his steak, drank his wine, and thought it over.

After a while, he dropped his utensils, mopped his mouth, and pushed away the rolling table, pushed it so vigorously as to tip the tiny bud vase with its single drooping orchid.

Leaning to his right, he opened the drawer of his night table and grabbed the knife he kept always within reach. It was long and slender with a brushed edge and a razor point, good for filleting and concealment. The plastic handle was flat and unobtrusive. The narrow blade slid smartly into a supple leather sheath; when he wore it on his person it barely made a bulge in his sock.

He admired the weapon a moment, then leaped the short distance between his small feet and the floor. Theatrically, he paused before moving with the measured steps of a toreador toward Katy's suitcase, still propped up on its stand. Knife in hand, he contemplated her lingerie, then leaned into a slow and lewd assault upon it.

He lifted up a lacy bra, severed the well-formed cups one from the other. He raised a translucent red negligee, vented it at chest and tummy. He skewered panties, halved thongs into the shapes of slingshots. He wrestled with stockings, tatters of nylon falling around him like dark snow. In his gradually accelerating fury, unsprung clasps and ribbons of spandex were tossed around the room.

Titillated by his deranged exertions, Big Al broke into a rutting sweat. He destroyed a final garter belt, murdered a last chemise, then threw himself into an armchair and surveyed with pleasure the black and pastel mess he'd made. Let her come back, he thought, and find *that.*

In the next heartbeat he edited the thought; in fact, erased it. He wasn't thinking about her coming back. He didn't want her to come back. He was over it already. He was moving on.

He'd be going out tonight. Hitting the bars. Pick up a sex-starved tourist or, failing that, a hooker. Get back on track, vacationwise. And, just in case his former girlfriend Katy happened to swing by to retrieve her things, let her find him with someone else. Let her see how easily replaced she was, how little she'd really mattered.

Katy and Al Tuschman finished up their dinner, then lingered over coffee to hear the island music and watch the chickens scratching in the dirt.

By the time they left the courtyard, it was well after nine. Heading for Duval Street, they slowly pedaled their borrowed bikes through air the temperature of skin. Katy now and then heard airplanes flying in and flying out, wondered which one she was supposed to be on. She was surprised at herself for staying; more surprised to have been invited. Now and then she stole a look at Al, wobbling along beside her with his dog in his basket. Straightforward, decent, he was just the sort of man she'd forgotten how to understand. Grateful for his gallantry, she told herself that when they parked the bikes and walked, it would be nice to take his arm. But she doubted she would really do it because she doubted that he wanted her to. That's how much she didn't understand him.

Duval Street was crowded and it gleamed with the ghoulish colors of humming neon. Drunks weaved among tourists trying to be drunk. Southern girls strutted by in tight lace shirts, their piled hair fighting off the dampness.

Al and Katy locked their bikes to a tree. Al bent down to tie his shih tzu to a parking meter. The dog looked at him with resignation and maybe just a hint of blame. They picked a bar more or less at random.

The place had music but no dancing. After a while Katy tapped Al on the back of his hand. He was looking at the bandstand, he hadn't expected to be touched, and he jumped a little bit. "Still wanna dance?" she shouted.

He did, but the truth was that his nerve had been eroding. Dancing at Coco's was one thing—it had just happened. Now he was *planning* to dance. This was different. "First let's have another drink," he shouted back.

Around eleven they were on the sidewalk once again. Retrieved the yawning dog. Left the bikes and strolled up the still-mobbed street. Katy thought to take Al's arm but didn't. After a couple of blocks they saw, reflected on parked cars and café umbrellas, the edgy, shattered light of a disco ball. They traced the flecks of glare to a second-floor club above an outdoor restaurant. Katy looked at Al. Al swallowed hard, wrapped Fifi's leash around a bike rack.

They went upstairs and danced. Danced like Al hadn't danced in many years, and like he never thought his grinding knees and gnarly ankles would let him dance again.

They left around one-thirty. A red moon was low in the west.

Fifi was tangled in her leash and sulking. They reclaimed their bikes and shakily headed home toward Paradise, much too tired and too secretly nervous at being roommates to notice the Jaguar parked across from the hotel in the ragged shadow of the buttonwoods.

Big Al Marracotta's evening had not been going all that well.

He'd been in several bars, and he was fairly drunk before he'd started. But he'd made a plan and he was sticking to it. For the sake of both economy and sport, he'd decided to give it until midnight to find some sex he wouldn't have to pay for. Your basic pickup. Sex with a lonely visitor who needed her cigarette lit, who was waiting for her package tour to be made complete.

But with this stratagem he'd gotten nowhere. Women kept turning their backs on him. Big Al wasn't used to this. The places he went to in New York—they were Mob places, and he was recognized, if not by name, at least by type. The women there were looking for that type. This made Al mistakenly imagine that he was attractive. But these tourist women—from Iowa, from Ontario—what did they know from Mafia? Too ignorant to be impressed with what he did, they saw him only for what he was: a short gruff pushy guy with shiny shoes.

After midnight he started looking for a hooker. To his surprise, this turned out to be not so easy either. Again, it was a question of style. Al's eyes were peeled for a good old-fashioned New York whore: the slinky one-zip dress, the blowjob lipstick, the stockings with their dark tops showing just a little. Al couldn't seem to find that type, though he looked in several likely joints, and had a few more drinks in the process. Stumbling now on a sidewalk no longer horizontal, he wandered toward the oceanfront, looking for a floozy by the seawall. Nothing doing.

Once more he staggered up Duval Street. A fleeting spasm of wisdom came to him in the guise of nausea, told him he was probably too smashed to function anyway, and he may as well go back to his hotel. But just then, half a block away, he spotted a woman who came very close to his ideal. She was tall. Her skirt was short, her stockings obvious. In silhouette her chest made a long grade to the summit. She was standing outside a bar that Al had missed, finishing up a cigarette. She met his eye; he was sure she did. She dropped the butt on the sidewalk, snuffed it out with a twist of high-heeled shoe that refreshed Big Al's libido, and sashayed back inside.

He followed her in, moved through close-packed tables, and found her at the bar. As was right and fitting, she was unsurprised to see him. Not without some difficulty, he climbed onto a barstool next to her. "Buy you a drink?"

"I love that opening," she said.

Al didn't take the sarcasm personally. Sass was part of the routine. He liked it. He gestured toward the bartender. They ordered drinks and he sized her up. Good wig but arousingly fake, blond above dark brows. Thick, cakey bands of eyeliner continuing past the edges of her eyes. Powdered cleavage delving into tempting shadow.

The drinks came. Al said, "Ya don't mind, let's get down to business."

"Can we have a toast at least?" the hooker said. Rather forcefully, she clinked his glass. "Bottoms up."

They drank. Al said, "I want the whole night and I don't want no to anything. How much?"

The hooker let her cold glass rest against her lip a moment. "Five hundred."

"That's big-city prices," Al observed.

"So? You wanna get fucked or you wanna ride the subway?"

Al looked down at the hooker's backside. "Riding the subway doesn't sound like such a bad idea."

"Five hundred. Free transfer."

"Deal," said Al. "Let's go." Gingerly, he started climbing down.

The hooker didn't budge. "Can't a girl even finish her drink?"

Grudgingly, Big Al climbed up again. The sudden change of direction made him just a little dizzy. He sipped his drink, and somewhere between the sip and the swallow he got the first inkling that something was not exactly right. He couldn't put his finger on it. He looked at the hooker. There was something a little too playful at the corners of her mouth. He glanced all around the bar. He liked tall women but this looked like a hoops squad. Redheads whose necks were on the thick side, brunettes with voices huskier than average. And there was something in the air, something barely smellable beneath the layers of flowery perfume, an elusive whiff of mannish sweat.

Big Al dropped his slurring voice. "You sure you're a woman?"

The hooker said, "Honey, I'm all the woman you can handle."

She said it a little louder than it needed to be said, and it dawned on Al that she wanted other people to hear it, that other people had been listening all along. Through a fog of alcohol he dimly realized that this was not the normal sass, that he was being mocked. His lips pulled taut across his teeth and his hairline started itching. "Don't fuck with me," he said.

The hooker gave an unafraid, coy shrug that really pissed him off.

With his chin he gestured toward her crotch. "I find a dick down there, I swear ta Christ I'll cut it off."

"*Now* you tell me, sweetie. Cost me a Miata to have a fancy surgeon do that very thing."

Big Al Marracotta blinked, and in the blink he was visited by a terrifying image of a hairy ersatz vulva between two hairy thighs. What was it made of? Pig intestine? Scrotum skin? Where did it lead? He said to the hooker, "You fucking faggot."

"Yeah, ain't it grand?" she said, and threw the rest of her drink in his face.

It took Big Al a moment to react. Then, eyes burning, cheeks dripping, he reached down blindly toward the knife he carried in his sock. But before his fingers could find the handle, the hooker grabbed him by the shirtfront and shoved him backward, stool and all. To Al, it felt like he was strapped securely in his seat but the airplane had disintegrated. His head snapped forward then back, his knees had somehow got above his face, he saw the ceiling skating past like a nightmare of galloping sky. He tucked and felt his stomach slide up toward his throat and waited for the sickening collision with the ground.

Two six-foot drag queens caught him just before he hit the floor. Putting dignity aside, he rolled off the stool onto his hands and knees, then scrambled to his feet. His legs trembled and his head was pounding and his innards churned. He longed to punch someone but didn't dare. A large and perfumed group had gathered all around him. Their heaving and emphatic bosoms left him barely room enough to wobble toward the door.

26

Al Tuschman hadn't brought pajamas. Katy Sansone had no clothes except the ones she was wearing. They tried not to acknowledge a certain awkwardness as they prepared for bed.

Brushing her teeth with an index finger, Katy examined the outdoor shower and said through toothpaste, "Hey, Tusch, y'ever go to sleepaway camp?"

He was washing his face, reaching for a towel. "Coupla summers. Sports camp, mostly."

"Me, I never did. Always wanted to. Crickets. Marshmallows. Canoes. Ya have canoes?"

Al looked at her. Her eyes were sleepy and her mouth had softened with fatigue. There was an intimacy in seeing someone so frankly tired. They kept talking because they couldn't stand to have the intimacy of silence added to it.

"Canoes," he said. "A raft you could swim to in the middle of the lake. Steps were slimy. Squished between your toes."

He sidled out of the bathroom. In the armoire by the picture of the greenish women with the greenish breasts, he found an extra pillow and a light blanket. He took them over to the sofa in the alcove. Fifi, exhausted and confused, followed him and sniffed at the upholstery. Al turned off the light. Skulking in shadow, he stripped to his jockey shorts and lay down. The sofa was not quite as long as he was, but if he curled his legs it wasn't bad. The dog jumped up and settled in against his feet.

He heard the toilet flush. A wedge of light came through the bathroom door then was extinguished. Katy padded toward the bed; Al could tell her shoes were off. He didn't want to hear it, but he heard the zipper of her shorts. He heard the soft tick of buttons as she laid her blouse over the back of a chair. The bed squeaked a little when she sat down on it, and he could not help wondering if the sheets felt cool or warm against the backs of her long legs. He heard her swivel and lie down. He was relieved to think that by now the cotton blanket was pulled up beneath her chin.

After a moment, she said, "Tusch?"

"Yeah?"

"I think it's really great you're letting me stay here. I think it's really great we danced."

Trying to sound more sleepy than he felt, Al said, "I'm glad you're here."

"Really?"

"Really. Go to sleep."

She was silent for a moment. A soft breeze lifted the curtains from the windowsills.

"Tusch?"

"Yeah?"

"Hear the crickets?"

"I think those are tree frogs."

"Hey, I'm from Queens. G'night."

The sheets rustled once and then Katy seemed to be asleep. Al lay there for a while in his gallant curl. Then he reached down and dragged the dog underneath the blanket till it was nestled in between his arms and chest, and drifted off himself.

Outside in the Jag, Chop Parilla said, "So, Squid, we don't get fancy, right?"

Sid Berman didn't answer, didn't even look Chop's way. He was gathering his concentration, and besides, killing people made him irritable. He didn't like it at all. This was a matter not of sentiment but taste. Other crimes evolved, unfolded. They had a flow to them, a music. But murder was a blank brick wall that stopped the band, destroyed the flow, forced an ending that, by necessity, was always too abrupt. This depressed him.

Edgy, Chop Parilla went on. "You're in, spear 'im, you're out again, I drive away, we're finished. Right?"

"Right," said Berman grudgingly.

It was getting on toward 3:00 A.M. The moon had dimmed to a mauve smudge and set. The streets were quiet except for the electric hum of the streetlamps and a very occasional howl or cackle from a passing drunk. The air had cooled just enough for a patina of condensation to form on the windshields of parked cars.

"What about the broad?" said Chop.

"What about 'er?"

"I don't like it there's someone with him."

"Picked up a chippy. Getting laid before he dies. I think that's kinda nice."

"Nice we got a witness?"

"Chop," said Squid, "imagine this. You've just fucked a guy. Next thing you know he's got a fish stuck through his heart. You gonna notice much besides the fish?"

Chop frowned, drummed fingers on the steering wheel. "I just wish he was alone."

Squid was getting exasperated. "You're the one so anxious to get finished. Ya want we do 'im tonight or ya want we don't?"

Chop just squeezed his lips together.

But all at once Squid was ready, and with the readiness came an awful thrill he could no longer deny. He felt it behind his knees and underneath his tongue.

Swallowing deep, he opened the glove compartment, reached for his powdered rubber gloves, and pulled them on. From underneath his seat, he produced a cylinder of pepper spray, stuck it in the waistband of his pants. "Come on," he said, "it's time."

Chop petted the dashboard then started the Jag, eased it over to the hotel entrance, and sat there softly idling.

Squid pulled a cut-off stocking down over his face. The nylon squashed his nose and tugged at the corners of his eyes, exposed the red rims of his eyelids. He slipped out of the car, reached into the backseat, and retrieved the stuffed fish with the two-foot spike of a nose. He bounced the pad of his index finger against the tip of it. "Fucker's sharp," he said to Chop.

Chop said nothing, just sat there scanning the street with his passenger door wide open.

Squid slipped through the gate of the hotel, darted into the shadow of an oleander, and took a moment to survey the courtyard. Soft blue light hovered as though it were a solid thing above the pool. Empty lounges were arranged in friendly groupings. Wisps of mist escaped from the edges of the hot tub cover.

He looked toward the office. The light was on, the door was open, and he had no choice but to pass quite near it. He took a deep breath, held it. Hunkering low, the fish under his arm, he scooted by the doorway. Out of the corner of his eye he saw the sleeping desk clerk, elbows on the counter, cheeks resting in his palms.

Squid jogged around the still-damp apron of the pool until he reached the gravel path overgrown with giant philodendrons. Small stones crunched beneath his feet, but nothing stirred as he slipped around to the side of Big Al's bungalow and stood in the darkness near the thatch enclosure of the shower. Through the mesh that muffled his nose and mouth, he sniffed the air, freighted with chlorine and salt and iodine. He practiced his grip on the fish. With his right hand around the narrow place just before the tail, he could use his left to guide the thrust. The fish weighed six, eight pounds and would make an admirable harpoon.

He got the pepper spray ready to immobilize the dog.

Then he crawled beneath the thatch onto the wet slats of the shower. He scrabbled to his feet and tried the bathroom door.

Unlocked as always. He let himself in. Smelled soap and tooth-paste and deodorant. Gave his eyes a moment to adjust to the deeper darkness inside the bungalow, then sidled toward the doorway to the bedroom.

Squinting, straining, he studied the bed as though there were some mystic pattern in the rise and fall of the ripples in the cotton blanket. He knew there were two bodies there. He knew that any second the dog would start to yelp and time would shrink to a twitch and he'd have to take his shot. But meanwhile he could see no more than one inchoate lump between the sheets, one heap suggesting tangled limbs and loins.

Readying the fish, he edged closer, his knees nearly touching the foot of the bed, close enough to hear the whoosh of breath. And from this new perspective, the geometry of the bedclothes told him there was just one person on that mattress. Was it possible? It made sense that the chippy would do her business and then slip out. So much the better. But how had she got past them, watching in the Jag?

No time to think about it now.

He inched up along the bedside, following the cocoon that swathed Big Al from heel to head, passing knees, thighs, waist, measuring the distance to the victim's rib cage, to the heart and lungs that would be pierced. He started lifting the fish. Its lac-quered skin had gotten sticky from the heat of his gloved fingers.

He raised the tail above his head. He balanced the abdomen against his other hand so that the death-spike pointed toward Big Al's torso at an angle like a falling bomb. He caught a sharp breath through the nylon that deformed his face, hitched his arms a notch higher, then locked his bandy muscles, fixed his gaze on the lump of flesh about to die, and brought the stuffed fish hurtling down with all his might.

At that instant Katy Sansone twitched the sheet back from her face.

Squid Berman saw the spiky hair, the forehead that was not Big Al's, and was horrified.

The harpoon was heavy, was descending with a dread momentum. This was a debacle. There was nothing artful about killing the wrong person, skewering a chippy. But the spike was coming down and he didn't have the strength to stop it. All in a heartbeat he was wrestling against the very motion that he'd started, his limbs contending wildly against themselves. He clamped down with his arms, tried to suck back gravity with the muscles of his chest, and managed just barely to deflect the grim trajectory of the spike.

It sliced through the blanket and grazed Katy Sansone's flank before sticking eyes-deep in the mattress, impaled as though it had fallen from the sky.

Squid Berman, his balance thrown off in the grotesque and desperate effort to change the course of wrongful murder, fell flat on top of Katy, pushed off again and started running even as she screamed.

Her scream, at last, woke up the dog, which had been insulated from sound and foreign odors by her master's blanket and his breathing and the safe smell of his chest. But now, hair on end, with no thought whatsoever for herself, the valiant shih tzu sprang down from the sofa and lit out on ticking, sliding paws toward the intruder. She caught up with him as he was escaping through the bathroom door. He paused just long enough to shoot pepper at her nose and eyes, then crawled beneath the shower and was gone. Fifi yelped and ran in circles.

Al Tuschman bolted up as well, as quickly as his cramped legs would allow, and ran the short length of the alcove. Groping for the switch, he turned the light on and discovered, through the rude and sudden glare, a bizarre and inexplicable tableau: a painted sailfish having done a face-plant through his mattress, and Katy quivering like an outsized butterfly freshly pinned in wax.

"Jesus. You okay?" he asked.

She couldn't answer right away. She was trembling and she badly needed to slip out from under the pole-axed blanket, to persuade herself she wasn't really trapped there.

The dog, in torment, found Al's feet, whimpered piteously against his ankles.

He picked her up and stroked her head, and watched the pale and quaking Katy wriggle toward the edge of the sheet.

To no one in particular he said, "God Almighty. And I really thought my luck was changing."

THREE

27

Al Tuschman stood inside the thatch enclosure and held his dog high up beneath a tepid shower. Fifi didn't like the splash and dribble of the water but it was better than the burn of pepper. She trusted that her master was doing the right thing.

Katy Sansone was leaning against the counter by the sink. With a pale green washcloth she dabbed at the thin line of drying blood that stained her right side, just above the waist.

It was three-thirty in the morning. Adrenaline had rendered them wide awake and almost sober. Calamity was intimate but not immediately sexy; they felt hardly any discomfort now, standing in their underwear.

Turning off the shower, wrapping the wet dog in a bath towel, Al said, "Didja see anybody? Anything?"

Katy shook her head, kept dabbing at the blood. The thin red line would disappear and then re-form, a little fainter every time. "Someone fell on top of me. That's all I felt. Didn't even feel the cut. Didn't see a thing."

Rubbing the dog in the towel, Al said, "Maybe the clerk."

They retreated to their separate corners, retrieved their clothes, and dressed. The stuffed fish was still poised in its improbable headstand on the bed, its spined fin spread proudly open like a winning hand of cards. They left it there as evidence.

Outside, the layer of blue light still sat atop the pool. Giant leaves secretly savored the hours of dripping dew. Al carried Fifi as he and Katy crunched over the gravel to the office.

They found the desk clerk dozing with his elbows on the desk. A tiny muted television threw an anemic glare on one side of his face. With a considerate softness, Al said, "Excuse me . . ."

If the clerk heard him at all, he heard him in a dream. A mouth corner tightened, ruby studs moved on his eyebrow.

Louder, Al said, "Excuse me!"

The clerk blinked himself awake.

"Did you just see someone sneak in and out of here?" Al asked him.

"Hm?"

Al put his hands flat on the counter, leaned across them. "Look. Someone just broke in here with a giant fish and tried to kill her. I'm asking if you saw anyone."

Sleepily the clerk said, "Giant fish?"

Al said, "You are really worthless."

People are sensitive when they first wake up. The desk clerk flushed and for an instant seemed about to cry. "You don't have to get nasty, Mr. Tuschman. I've worked eight straight shifts."

"I know, I know," said Al, feeling guilty now. "Rents are high. How 'bout you call the cops for us, at least."

The clerk stifled a yawn then reached stiffly toward the phone. His hand was lifting the receiver when Katy softly said, "No."

Al looked at her in her pink shorts and lime-green blouse and high-heeled sandals. "No?"

Katy's near-demise had focused her attention, and she'd been thinking hard. She'd been thinking about nicknames. About license plates. About how that other Al was treated in the seafood restaurants they used to go to in the city. "Tusch," she said, "I think we better talk."

"Mafia?" said Alan Tuschman. The word felt odd in his mouth, felt like a stranger had borrowed his voice to say it.

Katy blew steam from the surface of her coffee. "I mean," she said, "you never know for sure. But, hey."

She broke off with a shrug and Al looked out the window, checked on Fifi, tied up to a parking meter. They were sitting in an all-night diner on Duval. The bars had just closed and there was something bleakly, forsakenly transitional about the scene outside. It could almost have been quitting time in a mill town somewhere. People wandered, glazed, unsatisfied, wondering what was left for them to do with the dregs of time until they slept. Cop cars cruised by slowly, waiting for the sluggish, drunken fights to start.

Katy went on. "This much I know—he was having business troubles in New York. That's what all of a sudden put him in such a rotten mood. Whoever he works for, they put his worst enemy in charge. That bent him really outa shape."

Al played with his spoon and thought it over. "I just don't see what this poor bastard's business troubles have to do with you almost getting murdered."

Katy sipped her coffee. Out in the unnatural twilight of the sidewalk, two guys started cursing at each other. Softly, she said, "Tusch—or should I say Big Al?—who was supposed to be in that bed?"

Al blinked. He plucked at his shirtfront, twisted his neck from one side to the other. He ran his hands over his torso where the spike would have gone in. "Now wait a second . . ."

Katy waited several seconds, but Al could not continue right away.

Finally, with the brittle logic of someone trying to convince himself, he went on. "Look. He's from New York, I'm from Jersey. He's in seafood, I sell furniture. He's like five foot two, I'm six foot three. Someone mixed us up? . . . Nah, it's too ridiculous."

"Okay, it's ridiculous," said Katy. She paused as a waitress went by with a cinnamon roll. The cinnamon smelled great. "Mind I get a Danish?"

"Get a Danish."

She ordered it and then resumed. "So, Tusch, okay, it's ridiculous. But lemme ask you something. Do you have friends or enemies who are the kind of people who would put rotten calamari in someone's car?"

"No."

"He does."

The Danish arrived. She cut it into wedges and started eating one.

"Lemme ask you something else. Among your circle of acquaintances, are there guys who specialize in finding weird new ways to murder people in their beds?"

Al pulled on his face. It had been a long night and the skin felt very loose. Absently, he picked up and chomped a piece of Danish, swallowed it along with the conclusion he could no longer fend off. "It's one big fat mistake?" he murmured. "The whole thing's been one big fat mistake?"

Katy shrugged and sipped her coffee.

Al sipped his, then suddenly brought forth a quick and honking chuckle. He tried to put some sportsmanship in it but that didn't work. "I don't know whether to laugh or be really pissed."

She looked at him over the rim of her cup. "Be pissed. It might come in handy."

She said it as an ally. He knew she did, but still, the comment worried him. She saw the worry in his face.

"Look," she went on, "I know a little bit about these people. They're bullies. Real tough till you stand up to them."

"Stand up to them?" said Al. "They're killers. Me, I haven't had a fight since junior high."

"Come on. You're big. You're strong."

"I'm chicken."

He tried to say it lightly, blithely, but at 4:00 A.M. things have a way of coming out truer than they are really meant to. Katy's face told Al that his joke had failed but his revelation had succeeded. He prepared to flush with embarrassment. But he looked at Katy's unmocking eyes, and the embarrassment didn't come. He felt relief instead. He heard himself keep talking.

"I've always been chicken. Playing sports. The pressure, the contact, you could get wracked up any second. Always scared. Never admitted it. Can't admit it if you're big. Some people see right through it, though. Like my boss. Ya know what he told me just as I was leaving to come down here? Told me, 'Al, you're big, you're strong, but deep down you're a softie.' Killed me with that."

Katy said, "I think it's nice."

"Nice," said Al dismissively. "Nice for selling dinettes. Less nice for dealing with the Mafia."

Katy started picking up another piece of Danish, put it down again, and placed her hand on top of Al's. Her hand was a little sticky but he liked it. "Tusch," she said, "everyone's afraid. Doesn't matter you're afraid, matters what you do."

It mattered to him. He looked at her and frowned. Outside, a patrol car had turned its beacon on; cold blue light raked across the diner window. Fifi had started barking.

"You'll do what needs doing," she told him. "I know you will."

He doubted it. He said, "How's your side? It hurt?"

"No big deal," she said. "Hey—how 'bout we find someplace to watch the sun come up?"

28

On Long Island, dawn was on a dimmer, the sun thwarted like an unlucky performer who couldn't find the break in the curtain. Light barely trickled through a chilly haze the color of weak tea. It was an hour before there was brightness enough to quell the streetlamps and throw the first, faint shadows from basketball hoops and minivans crouched in asphalt driveways.

In his four-bedroom split-level, Nicky Scotto woke up nervous. He tried to convince himself that it was a happy nervous, the nervousness that came with triumph. Big Al Marracotta should be dead by now. If everything had gone well, that is. His own control of the fish market should be secure—assuming he'd rightly interpreted Tony Eggs' sphinxlike advice.

But what if he hadn't?

Too late, the rashness and the riskiness of his strategy was getting through to Nicky. He'd unilaterally called a hit on a powerful and well-connected man. Cagey old Tony had stopped well short of saying anything that would make him party to the call; he could totally disclaim it with a shrug, a lifted eyebrow. What if something went wrong? What if it was only his ambition that made Nicky imagine that he'd got the go-ahead?

He tried not to think about it. He showered and shaved and dressed for work.

But at the fish market office, his antsiness only increased. Big Al's things were still around. The edges of his family portraits stuck out from underneath the phone books. His calendar had a dentist's appointment marked down on it. This gave Nicky the creeps, brought home to him the enormity of what he'd set in motion.

Besides, he could not get comfortable in his cheap new suit. The rough wool chafed him behind the knees. The stiff sleeves bound him at the elbows. His lapels would not lie flat, and he could not banish the thought that when he saw guys whose lapels stuck out like that, he thought of them as pissants.

The morning went very slowly. He kept waiting to be summoned to the pay phone across the yard, to get the news that his nemesis had in fact been iced. He tugged on his lapels. The call didn't come.

Finally, around ten-thirty, he broke down and decided to get in touch with Florida.

He left the office, went outside, trudged through oily puddles and around the loading dock, and lifted the freezing-cold receiver to his ear. Inhaling diesel, exhaling steam, he dialed. The phone rang a long time and then a sleepy Chop said, "Yeah?"

"So what's the story?"

"Nicky?"

"No, Santa Claus. Didja do 'im yet?"

Chop struggled up onto an elbow, used his other hand to rub his eyes. "Well, not exactly."

"Fuck is not exactly? Ya did 'im or ya didn't."

"We tried," Chop said. "He wasn't in his bed. Some broad was there."

Nicky could not help being curious. "Tall broad?"

"How you know?"

"Lotta attitude? Kathy, Kitty, somethin' like that?"

"Squid went in wit' a stocking on his head," said Chop. "I don't think they chatted."

Nicky did a little dance to warm his feet. "Okay, okay. So when ya gonna try again?"

Dryly, Chop said, "I guess when Squid wakes up."

There was a pause. Nicky shivered and tried to figure why his cheap new suit made him sweat indoors but didn't keep him the least bit warm outside. Must be a fucking blend.

"Nicky," Chop went on at last, "this isn't turning out to be as easy as you think it is."

"Come on. The guy's on his own, ya know where he is—"

"Squid won't use a gun or a knife."

"So let 'im use a wire, an ice pick—"

"He won't use anything but seafood."

"Say wha'?"

"Seafood. He started the job wit' seafood, he says he won't finish any other way. Last night's try was wit' a sailfish."

"Sailfish?"

"Stuffed. Ya know, the nose."

"For Christ's fucking sake," said Nicky.

"You wanted a genius," said Chop. "You got one."

Nicky chewed his lip, wrapped himself in the cold, metal housing of the phone wire. "Chop, I ain't got time for this. Tell Squid—"

"I've told him," Chop interrupted. "The fucking guy's impossible. I don't know what he's gonna do. Get a octopus ta strangle 'im? Give 'im a heart attack wit' men-a-war?"

Nicky finally realized that, on top of his frustration, he was getting very scared. He'd hired lunatics and they were blowing it. His plot would be discovered and he'd be sure as hell rubbed out. Every hour that passed increased the chances it would go that way. In a pinched, congested voice, he said, "I want him done today. Today."

Chop said calmly, "Nicky, I'm bein' as straight wit' you as I can be. All I can promise you is seafood. I can't promise you today, I can't promise you tomorra—"

Nicky Scotto slammed down the phone, slammed it down with such gusto that he felt the lining in the right shoulder of his cheap new suit begin to tear.

In the narrow bed across from Chop's, Squid Berman was still pretending to be asleep. But he couldn't quite hide that he was smiling. He was winning. He was happy. He was doing things his way and not letting anybody spoil it.

Big Al Marracotta had had worse outings, but they'd generally entailed someone ending up in a car compactor or a garbage dump. For an occasion not involving death, the misery of this last night would be hard to top.

Humiliated in the drag bar, he'd staggered up Duval Street, back toward his hotel. But his nerves were shaken, and he needed one more drink. He had it, then resumed his journey. His legs were tired, however; the walk seemed long, and he decided to break it up by stopping for another cocktail. By 4:00 A.M. he was within two blocks of the Conch House. Cruelly, the lights came up in the last place that would serve him, and he threw himself into the meandering stream of diehards on the sidewalk. Surrounded by taller men, unseeing and unseen, he'd stumbled right past the glaring window of an all-night diner. A stupid little dog had singled him out to bark at.

Back in his room at last, he took some aspirin and immediately threw up. Rising from the bowl, he'd wandered to the bedroom and walked around in dizzy circles, looking down at the tattered shreds of Katy's underthings. Then he'd passed out, small and alone and smelling foul, on the huge bed meant for frolicking.

He awoke now to a shard of late-morning sun slicing through the drapes and a monumental hangover. His eyeballs had dried out, his cheeks stuck to his gums. His kidneys felt like they had sugar crystals deep inside them. He put a pillow on his head but could not get back to sleep. Finally he called room service, ordered every purported cure that he could think of. Tomato juice. Oysters. Soft-boiled eggs.

In the agony of waiting for his breakfast, he tried but failed to fend off a terrible admission: vacation, all in all, was going lousy.

For a rare and blurry introspective second, he wished he could pinpoint and repair the moment it had all gone wrong, but he knew that he could not. He'd lost his girlfriend and he felt like hell. He was bored stiff with lying in the sun. Business problems were preying on his guts and he saw no way to turn the thing around.

The embarrassing truth was that he might as well go home. Back to wife and work and aggravation, back to the stinking weather and the smell of fish.

He just had to find a way to explain it to himself, and to others, so that it wouldn't look like he had caved, so that leaving early wouldn't feel like a defeat. Once he'd figured that one out, he was ready to get on the road.

29

Katy and Al Tuschman had finished their coffee, then retrieved the dog and gone to the pier at County Beach to watch
the sun come up.

They'd sat on rough boards damp with night, their feet dangling above an ocean so still that it reflected pale blue stars amid
the gold-green streaks of phosphorescence. For a moment Katy's
head had rested on Al's shoulder. He didn't know if she had
meant to put it there or if she'd briefly nodded out. He'd
thought to touch her hair, but didn't. He'd stroked the dog instead.

Just after six, the eastern sky had turned a rusty yellow and
swallowed up the constellations. Narrow, scattered slabs of cloud
went lavender, and the water changed from black to a strange
and depthless burgundy. When the sun cracked the horizon, it
was instantly too bright to look at. The air grew hot in seconds
and the tropic day came on so suddenly that there was no way to
be ready for it. Caked sand sparkled; shadows stretched away
from palms, opaque and confident, like they'd been there all
along.

Taken by surprise, Al had shaded his itching eyes and was
overtaken by a yawn. "What now?" he said.

Katy shrugged and yawned in turn. Pelicans flew by. Fifi stood
and stretched over her front paws.

Thinking aloud, Al went on, "We go back to the hotel, we're sitting ducks."

Katy had squinted against the glare that skipped across the ocean like a spray of pebbles. "Maybe that's not the worst idea."

"Maybe not the best."

"Face them," she went on. "Explain things, get it over with."

Al thought about the fish stuck in the bed. "If you get time to explain."

Katy yawned again. It was a deep, sinuous yawn that made her feel the cut on her side. "Probably they won't do anything daytime."

Big, strong Al Tuschman considered that, then said, "What's the argument against bolting? Fleeing? Running away?"

For that Katy had no answer she could put in words. She just looked at Al with intimately tired eyes, and he understood, though he couldn't say it either. The only argument against fleeing was that if they bolted now they would lose each other. He'd get a flight to Newark, she to LaGuardia, and since they were very different from each other and weren't lovers, that would be the end of it. That's what happened when vacation was over and real life reasserted its habits and limits and demands. After sunset and sunrise and sharing a room, after dancing, and talking in their underwear, they'd go back to being the selves that they were used to, and it would seem preposterous, impossible that they would hang around together. That was the only argument against bolting right this minute.

Al bit his lip, looked down at the twinkling ocean. Not totally persuaded, he said, "I guess they won't try anything in daylight."

They stood and stretched. Fifi shook herself, dried her damp fur in the hot morning sun. They strolled slowly back to Paradise, where they soon fell sound asleep, side by side, on shaded lounges near the pool.

A block and a half from the fish market, beneath a torn green awning on a bent and rusty frame, there was an Irish bar. It had a chrome steam table filled with cylinders of soggy vegetables, and a plastic slab where a man in a spattered apron carved hunks of fatty meat. The place smelled of cabbage and stale beer and in the lull before lunch hour it was a perfect place to talk.

In a booth way at the back, Nicky Scotto was leaning forward above a Heineken and saying, "I gotta go to Flahda. Right away."

"Don't do it," said Donnie Falcone, solemn in his big black overcoat.

"It's the only way," said Nicky. Desperation made him lean still farther.

Donnie leaned in too. Their noses were close. They could smell each other's aftershave. "Think. You can't be seen in Flahda. It's suicide. What about the guys you—"

"They're fucking up," said Nicky. "Unbelievably, they're fucking up. I gotta do the fuckin' job myself."

"You told me they were pros," said Donnie. "I don't see what's the—"

"Problem?" Nicky interrupted. Furiously he swigged some beer, wriggled against the booth to try and stop the itching from his cheap and crappy suit. "Here's the fuckin' problem." He told Donnie about his hired men's determination to finish the job with seafood.

"Jesus Christ," said Donnie, and he shook his head of beautiful black hair. "Where'd you find these guys?"

"Chop's solid," Nicky said. "Does cars in Hialeah. I've worked wit' 'im through Miami. But the other guy—Squid. He's good people but he's crazy."

Donnie rubbed his cardboard coaster; little tubes of paper rolled beneath his thumb. "Nicky, listena me. You cannot let yourself be linked—"

The other man locked his jaw to keep his voice from getting loud. "I'm runnin' outa time! How much longer's he gonna be down there? Two days? Three?"

"Nicky, please. Stay out of it. Let it run its course."

"They fuck it up," the man in the bad suit rambled, "and then what? Big Al gets outa Flahda. Comes back and takes over the market. Now he's surrounded wit' goombahs—"

"And you're no worse off than you were before," Donnie pointed out.

"Except I am," said Nicky. "'Cause I got my heart set on it. 'Cause in my mind it's done already."

"Nicky, please. I'm begging you—"

"I'm goin', Donnie. I got to. First plane I can get on."

Donnie pursed his lips and slowly pushed himself upright in the booth. He scratched an eyebrow and said, "Nicky, I got a question for you. From the very start a this whole fuckin' mess, every single thing I tell you not to do, you do it. Why you bother askin' my advice?"

Surprised by the question, Nicky blinked. He thought the reason should be obvious. Absently, he tugged at his gapping lapels. "'Cause you're my friend," he said.

30

After his late breakfast, Big Al Marracotta ate more aspirin, then pulled on his cabana set and went down to the pool. He simply didn't know what else to do.

But the midday sun ratcheted up the dull ache in his head until it was an unbearable throbbing, so he retreated into the shade and looked at women, shamelessly stared as they coaxed their bathing suits down over the pale crescents at the base of their buttocks, as they rearranged their bosoms after diving.

After a while he waded to the swim-up bar, had a Virgin Mary, and then another. He sucked the lemons, chewed the ice. Very gradually, the spices and the celery joined forces with the aspirin and made him feel a little better. He dunked his head in the pool, and the cool water seemed to siphon pain away. He ate an order of conch fritters. They expanded in his stomach and made him feel almost okay.

In its grim but loosening grip, the hangover now seemed less like an overwhelming fact than an arduous but necessary passage. On the far side of that passage lay something like peace of mind, in the form of several benign, face-saving fibs he could tell himself about vacation.

Sipping yet another Virgin Mary, he was beginning to believe it had all worked out for the best. He'd had a bunch of first-rate sex, then got rid of Katy without tears or complications. He was due to ditch her anyway; it was a good thing it happened now, so

he could have his blowout then get back to New York. Face it—
he was needed there. He counted. He was an important guy, and
nobody's patsy. He'd proven that by taking vacation when he
damn well wanted to. But now he'd be big about it, responsible,
and go home early. Impress the hell out of Tony Eggs with how
fast and neatly he could get the market back in order.

Resolved, almost happy, he waded out of the pool, reclaimed
his cabana jacket. He air-dried for a minute, then went up to his
room.

Upstairs, he sat down on the bed and tried not to realize he
was nervous. He studied the telephone, silently rehearsed. The
words, the tone of voice—it had to be exactly right. He breathed
deep and dialed Tony Eggs' social club.

An underling answered. The underling was allowed to pass
along the call only as far as Carlo Ganucci.

The old *consigliere* got on the line and said hello.

"Carlo!" said Big Al, bearing down to put some Florida sunshine in his voice. "How are ya?"

Ganucci's eyeballs had turned yellow and he was down to a
hundred fifteen pounds. He wasn't sure what was killing him
but he knew that he was dying. He said, "Fine. How're you?"

"Tan. Rested. Fabulous," said Big Al. "Tony there?"

Carlo tried to do his job. "Zere a message I can give 'im?"

"Please," said Al. "I'd really like to talk to 'im myself."

There was a pause. Ganucci figured that Tony probably didn't
want to be bothered with this call, but resisting, arguing, took
more strength than he could spare. He padded off to get the boss.

The line was vacant for what seemed to Al a very long time.
He strove to keep his concentration. Be upbeat, he told himself.
Cheerful. Strong.

Finally Tony Eggs picked up the phone. He didn't say hello.
He said, "So how's the weather down in Flahda?"

The sarcasm put a ding in Big Al's confidence. But he had a
game plan and he stuck to it. "Beautiful," he said. "Incredible.
But listen—"

"What ya got left down there?" Tony interrupted. "Two days? T'ree?"

"This is why I'm callin'," said Big Al. "I mean, it's great down here—the sun, the palm trees. But, hey, I got responsibilities. You got, like, a situation up there. I'm a guy does the right thing. So I'm comin' back early. Leavin' today."

Tony didn't answer right away. Big Al knew why. He was impressed. Grateful. Maybe even touched. Didn't know exactly what to say. Al basked in the silence, knowing that things had worked out for the best and he was scoring a lot of points.

At last Tony said, "Don't bother."

Big Al squirmed against the rumpled sheets. "Excuse me?"

"Don't bother. Take your time. Enjoy yourself."

Al squeezed out half a laugh that sounded sick. "Hey, that's nice a you, but my mind's made up. Where things stand wit' the market—"

"The market isn't your concern no more."

"What?" He jumped down from the bed, wrapped himself in phone cord.

Tony Eggs was very calm. "It isn't yours no more. I gave it back ta Nicky."

Numbly, Big Al echoed, "Gave it back to Nicky? Just like that?"

Tony said nothing.

"After the fuckin' job I did for you?"

"You did okay, Al," Tony Eggs conceded. "But your time there, it was, like, a tryout."

"A tryout? A fucking tryout? No one ever said anything about it bein' a tryout."

Tony put a shrug in his voice. "Well, that's what it was."

"Sonofabitch!"

"And inna meantime, Nicky convinced me just how bad he wanted it. Me, I like a guy who's hungry."

Big Al took tiny steps that led him in a circle. "I can't believe I'm hearin' 'iss."

"Believe it, Al," said Tony. "No hard feelins, huh?"

Marracotta tried and failed to keep a note of pleading out of his voice. "Don't do this ta me, Tony!"

"Enjoy the resta your vacation."

Big Al heard the phone click in his ear. He held the receiver at arm's length and stared at it a moment. His first impulse was to bash it against the wall, but he was suddenly too drained to do it. He replaced it gently in its cradle, sat down softly on the high edge of the bed.

In the social club on Prince Street, Tony Eggs Salento turned to his favorite nephew, Donnie Falcone.

Donnie said, "Thought fast on that one, *zìo.*"

Sorrowfully and mordantly the old boss shook his head. "Those guys are both such fuckin' losers."

In the courtyard at Paradise, Al and Katy had slept for hours as the other couples and the European threesome woke up and breakfasted, as the sun rose higher and tested their parasol of leaves and fronds.

They slept until the crisscrossed straps of their lounges had impressed their pattern on legs and arms and faces, and they now awoke among naked people basted with sunblock, breathing air perfumed with coconut and chlorine.

Katy yawned and stretched and rubbed the corners of her mouth. "Delicious sleep," she slurred. "Needed it. Delicious."

Cottony and not quite awake, carrying over some refrain from a vanished dream, Al Tuschman blinked at her and mumbled words that were mashed by the weight of his cheek against the lounge. "Mishin tibby hoppy."

"Hmm?"

With effort he rose up on a crampy elbow. Fifi squirted out from underneath his lounge and tried to lick his chin. He said, "People kept saying it to me when I first got here. 'Mission to be happy.' 'Happiness our mission.' Sounded stupid then."

Katy came up on an elbow too, and rearranged her blouse. "And now?"

He yawned and pulled his eyebrows close together. "Person doesn't just change," he said. "Score the basket. Close the sale. Ya know, those are missions."

"But you didn't answer the question," Katy pointed out.

"Yeah, I know I didn't," he admitted. Absently, he tugged his lower lip. The air felt great. Someone dunked in the pool and the water made a beautiful sound. Lizards clung to croton branches and billowed out their ruby throats. Al Tuschman gave an embarrassed little laugh. "Ya know," he said, "I think I sort of half believe it."

Katy reached across the space between their lounges and touched his hair. She didn't mean to do it; it just happened. His hair was dense and springy and a little moist from the heat of sleep. She quickly pulled her hand away and spoke immediately, as though to erase the fact that the touch had happened. "Mind I take a shower?"

He nodded and lay down flat again, thinking about her fingers in his hair, trying to forget that someone out there had in mind to make a dumb mistake and murder him. She went to the bungalow. The housekeeper apparently had been too shocked or baffled to make the bed. The stuffed fish, its blue and silver fin unfurled, still had its nose deeply buried in the mattress. Katy pulled it out. The nose offered a fair bit of resistance and made a creaking, scratching sound as it was withdrawn. The puncture in the sheet was neat and round.

She put the trophy on the dresser, then straightened out the tortured blanket and folded it neatly at the foot of the bed. At first she didn't know why she was bothering to do those things just then.

She stepped into the thatch enclosure and had a long warm shower.

When she went outside again, she was wearing a bathrobe that Al did not immediately recognize as his. The sleeves were rolled up to her elbows, the lapels were wrapped modestly around her throat. Her hair was wet and combed straight back and she hadn't bothered to put on makeup. She sat down on her lounge so that her knees were level with Al's chest.

He had to say something, so he said, "Nice shower?"

She didn't answer that. She said, "Tusch, I think it's time. Don't you?"

He knew what she was saying but he needed to be absolutely sure he knew. He'd started down the gallant path, and they probably should have fled by now, and as the hours passed he knew he should be getting more afraid; but he couldn't say or do a thing until he was absolutely certain what this tall young woman in his bathrobe was saying to him. So he just stared at her a moment.

She reached out and touched his hair again. "Time," she said again. "For us. Don't'cha think?"

31

Nicky Scotto's plane was just then landing in Miami, settling onto a tire-scarred runway that shimmered in the heat of afternoon.

In his sticky suit he hurried through the terminal, past pyramids of plastic oranges and mobs of South Americans checking in with televisions and Pampers boxes, and caught the jumper flight to Key West. It was a short flight but the attendant went through twice with drinks. People traveling in tank tops wolfed beers and margaritas out of cans, getting ready to be loud and silly.

Nicky thumbed a magazine, then looked out the window as the small plane started its descent. Where the flats began, the water of the Gulf thinned out from indigo to milky green; tide-scoured channels branched and meandered among the splotchy russet and maroon of coral heads. Colonies of mangrove sprouted inexplicably; gradually they thickened into islands, scraps of forest with their feet in swamps. Beautiful, thought Nicky. Lots of places to dump a body.

He caught a taxi at the airport and went straight to Chop's motel.

In the still-searing sun of four o'clock, he climbed a flight of outdoor stairs then knocked on the hollow, rotting door of the hired killers' room. The door was opened by a heavily sweating guy in a sleeveless T-shirt. Veins stood out in his neck and arms.

Nicky said, "You must be Squid."

"That's right," said the bandy man. He didn't offer his hand and he didn't smile.

Nicky tried a compliment. "Always heard good things about your work."

"When I get to do it," Squid said dryly. "Come in, ya want. I'm doin' calisthenics."

Nicky stepped over the threshold, closed the door behind him. Ignoring the guest, Squid dropped to the ratty carpet, started doing push-ups, the kind where you clap between each one.

"Where's Chop?" asked Nicky, sitting on a damp and musky unmade bed.

"He's doin' somethin'," grunted the man on the floor.

"He's workin' for me," said Nicky. "What's he doin'?"

"I don't really know," said Squid. He rolled onto his back and started doing sit-ups.

"I fuckin' told him when I'd be here," Nicky said.

Squid didn't bother answering that, and Nicky's irritation ripened quickly in the steamy climate. His two great hit men. One didn't have the decency to be there to greet him, and the other was an exercise freak who was giving him attitude. Where was the respect? Adding to his annoyance, the room was broiling hot and stank of mildew. He took off his jacket. His thin gray turtleneck was wet under the arms and along the spine. "This dump ain't got AC?"

Squid was curled up like a bug, hands behind his head, his left elbow reaching for his right knee. "While I'm sweated up?" he said. "You crazy?"

Nicky rose, started walking toward the bathroom to throw cold water on his face. Halfway there, his very fragile patience disappeared. "Am *I* crazy?" he said. "You wanna take a guy out wit' a stuffed fish hangin' on a wall, and you ask me if *I'm* crazy?"

Squid kept on with his crunches. With a quiet but implacable resentment, he said, "All I know is, ya hire guys to do a job, y'oughta let 'em do the job."

Nicky stood right over Squid. "Look, you seem to be forgetting whose job this is. For what I'm payin' you—"

Squid did not like looking at Nicky's crotch and up his nose. He sat and swiveled on his haunches. "You think this is about the money?"

Scotto was stumped by the question. What else could it be about?

"Fuck the money!" Squid went on, sitting lotus-style on the floor. "This is about symmetry. Completion."

Nicky blinked at him, scratched his ear, resumed his journey toward the bathroom.

"Fuck the money!" Squid repeated to his back. "The money for this hit, which now you're making about as elegant as a Kotex, fuhget about it. All I want's my per diem."

Nicky turned around. "Your per fucking what?"

The door opened. Light rolled into the room like a giant wedge of yellow cheese. Chop stepped in behind it and Nicky jumped right down his throat. "Where you fucking been?"

Unfazed, Chop said, "Picking out a spot. Ya know, for later. You guys been gettin' ta know each other?"

Big Al Marracotta had sat for a long time on the high edge of his hotel bed, sat there stunned, like a man amid the charred and tangled wreckage of what used to be his house. Too fast for sanity to track, everything was gone. Work; power; status; sex life— vanished. Just another aging middle-level wise guy once again. He stared at the wall and tried to get used to the idea.

Eventually he rose on numb legs and showered. He barely felt the water on his skin or the brisk rub of the towel.

Hiding in a hotel bathrobe, he walked in absent circles around his suite, tried out different armchairs. He noticed vaguely that the light outside was changing, turning golden. Soon it would be sunset. The big event of every day. Some event! Then again, at least it could not be taken away. In a morbid mood of anti-celebration, he decided he would leave his room to drink champagne as the sun was going down.

He got dressed. Stepped into sharkskin pants and, by force of habit, tucked his slender knife inside his sock before putting on his shoes. He combed his half-inch helmet of salt-and-pepper hair and headed for the rooftop bar.

Big Al was not a sentimental guy, had always moved too fast for nostalgia to catch up with him. Riding the elevator, smelling the sea, whose tang penetrated even to the airshaft, he didn't realize he was acting out an unamusing parody of his first evening in Key West. Reliving the sunset of just a few short days ago, when he'd been a big shot and a lover. Going back to the beginning, as though he could start vacation over and get it right this time.

Katy and Al Tuschman lay beneath the punctured blanket on the punctured bed and talked about their plans.

"Maybe South Beach for a coupla days," said Al. "Rent a car and drive right up."

Katy stroked his chest. She liked the way the whorls of hair wrapped themselves around her fingers. "You sure you wanna be with me that long?"

He ran a hand over the smooth rise of her hip. "Come on," he said. "Don't start that stuff. Coupla days in South Beach. Finish with a real vacation. Whaddya say?"

A breeze moved the thin curtains of the room. It was cooler than the breeze had been before and it lacked the brickish smell of high afternoon. The day was ending and the crazy, mistaken dangers of night were coming on.

"I say whatever we're gonna do, we better get started doing it."

She kissed him once then moved to get up from the bed. Al held her close a moment more, reveled in her length. Her toes tickled his insteps, their loins nested without contortion, her tanned cheek fit like a violin in the hollow of his neck.

He marveled once again at how smoothly she unfolded, as she rose to walk off toward the shower.

32

Across the street, in the lengthening shadow of the button-wood hedge, Squid was sulking in the backseat of the Jag. Chop sat observant and serene behind the steering wheel. Next to him, Nicky Scotto, jumpy and perspiring, kept plucking at his trousers, and gave off the funky acetone smell of a nervous man whose clothes were wrong for the tropics. He was very aware of the weight of the pistol Chop had given him; it pulled down on an inside pocket of his jacket and made him lean that way. He stared at the wooden gate of Paradise and said to no one in particular, "Ya sure he's coming out?"

"Fuck knows?" said Squid, enjoying the other man's discomfort. "Guy gets hungry, thirsty, he's comin' out."

Nicky prayed in secret that it would be soon. He could feel in his bowels that his nerve was wearing thin. He'd killed before, but never a made man. An equal. Someone with friends who solemnly believed in getting even.

Chop picked up where Squid left off. "Or if he has ta walk his little dog."

Nicky was plucking at his sticky pants and watching the shadows slowly stretch across the street. "Little dog?" he said. "He's got a big dog."

Chop Parilla felt just the faintest of misgivings but held his face together and said nothing, only looked across the street and drummed lightly on the steering wheel.

In the backseat, Squid Berman was taking a bleak pleasure from seeing more and more that the guy who wouldn't let him complete his masterpiece was a total idiot. Not bothering to mask his contempt, he said, "Have it your way, Nicky. Guy's got a big, gigantic dog."

"We're leaving," said Al Tuschman to the desk clerk with the ruby studs above his eye and the purple bags beneath them.

The drowsy fellow seemed indifferent yet confused. He glanced at the departing guest's suitcase, and at the woman who had not been with him when he'd arrived, and at the register before him on the counter. "You're booked for two more nights."

Al said, "I know that. We're going."

The clerk tried his best to look concerned. "Was everything all right?"

"No," said Al. "There's a gash in the mattress."

"A gash?"

"You might wanna think about security. Where can we rent a car right now?"

"Right now?" Time being featureless for him, he had to glance down at his watch. "Only place, the airport."

Putting his room key on the counter, Al said, "Would you call us a taxi, please."

He and Katy headed for the office door. Al held his suitcase and Katy held Fifi. The clerk watched them go, and could not help seeing some vague personal failure in their retreating backs. Through his exhaustion he rallied for one last burst of rote and insincere professionalism. "Please come back and see us!" he chirped.

Al looked across his shoulder. "Yeah, right."

But when he crossed the office threshold and stood for the last time in the courtyard with its pool and hot tub, its lounges where people rubbed and cooed and chattered, a strange thing happened: he suddenly felt a fondness for the place. In spite of everything, in spite of what, minute by minute, had felt like loneliness and awkwardness and misery, it now seemed to Al that he'd had a pretty good time there. He was tan and freshly showered. He'd caught up on his rest and had a tall new lover at his side. In some cockeyed, screwball way, vacation had turned out pretty well.

He took a last deep breath of chlorine and spent flowers, a last look at the closely tended palms with a yellow sunset glow behind them. He leaned close to Katy and kissed her on the neck, and then they headed for the wooden gate.

Across the street and thirty yards away, Chop Parilla watched as Al Tuschman dropped his suitcase and Katy bent down smoothly to put the leashed dog on the ground. He squeezed the wheel of the idling Jag and pointed with his big square chin. "There he is!" he hissed.

Nicky Scotto felt the urgency deep down in his guts. He narrowed his eyes and craned his neck. He squinted down, he stretched and strained, but finally he had to say, "There *who* is?"

In the backseat, Squid Berman chewed his tongue and thought, Is this guy a moron or what?

"Big Al!" said Chop.

Nicky tightened down his abdomen and rubbed his eyes and felt the gun against his ribs. He grabbed the dashboard and leaned far forward. "Where?"

Christ, thought Squid, the motherfucker's blind!

"Right there!" Chop said. "Wit' the tall broad and the dog!"

Nicky stared, and stared, and saw a stranger. A long and sweaty moment passed. Then he said, "Come on, don't fuck around."

For a heartbeat no one moved. Then Chop shifted very slightly in the driver's seat and slid his gaze to the rearview mirror, silently but desperately conferring with his partner.

Nicky tracked his eyes, saw the look on his face—hangdog,

crestfallen. In a nauseating instant, he understood. He said, "You fuckin' assholes! You think that's Big Al?"

"That *is* Big Al!" insisted Squid.

"You're telling me who Big Al is? I don't know that fuckin' guy from Adam!"

"The license plate—" said Chop.

"Fuck the license plate! Geniuses! Ya got the wrong guy all this time!"

Neither Chop nor Squid had anything to say to that. Chop just looked down at his knuckles. Squid thought ruefully about his brilliant work. Some masterpiece—wrong from the start.

"I tol' you," Nicky hammered on. "Little guy, big dog." He gestured toward the threesome quietly waiting for their taxi on the dusky sidewalk. "Zat look like a big dog ta you? Zat look like—"

He stopped himself mid-rant. Something had clamped on to his attention. A spiky head of raven hair above a pert, small-featured face above a healthy chest above a long thin pair of legs. He said, "Wait a second. Who's the broad?"

"You know everything," Sid Berman said. "You tell us."

"Come on, come on. Who is she?"

Chop shrugged. "Some broad that he picked up. Wasn't with 'im at the start."

Nicky looked harder. Long neck, slightly pointed chin. He'd seen her in New York. He was sure of it. At various bars and seafood joints. Sassy. Pouty. With a way of looking bored. He said, "Shit, I think that's Big Al's girlfriend."

Everybody was confused. Squid could not help saying, "Big Al's girlfriend. But not Big Al."

"Shut up," said Nicky. He plucked at his pants and tried to stitch his torn-up thoughts together. After a moment he said, "We're grabbing them."

Chop began, "But you just said—"

"Shut up. Go."

He put the idling Jag in gear.

22

Al and Katy had been talking about the great time they would have in South Beach. Long walks by the ocean. Cocktails in the crazy lobbies of old lime-green hotels. Finger food in suave cafés as beautiful people glided past on Rollerblades.

When the Jaguar stopped in front of them, Al tried to make a little joke. "Pretty fancy cab."

Katy smiled but did not have time to laugh. She looked up to see a suit moving toward her, caught a sickening glimpse of a big hand wrapped around a gun that gleamed a dull blue in the deepening dusk.

Squid spilled from the backseat right after Nicky. He bounded over to Al Tuschman and poked the muzzle of a pistol between his ribs.

Fifi barked. Nicky kicked her in the snout. He grabbed one of Katy's wrists and wrenched it behind her back and let her feel the gun against her spine. "Inna car," he whispered. "Not a fuckin' sound."

He used her long arm as a lever and pushed her to the Jag. She dragged the dog behind her; no one seemed to care.

Squid prodded Al Tuschman, who moved like he had just woken up. His suitcase, ghostly, stayed there on the sidewalk.

It happened too fast for real fear to grab on until they were seated in the car. That's when the milky feeling swelled up from the stomach, the cold burn moved down the legs. Al and Katy and the shih tzu were huddled in the back with Squid. Nicky swiveled toward them, his pistol poking lewdly through the slot between the bucket seats.

Chop drove away. Drove calmly, slowly. A sightseer's pace through peaceful, unsuspecting streets, past clapboard houses whose emerald and coral and turquoise shutters hoarded up the fading light.

Nicky said to Katy, "I know you." The simple statement was a horrid accusation. "Kitty. Kathy. You fuck Big Al. Am I right?"

Katy said nothing. By now she vaguely recognized her captor. One more thug from the thuggish places she used to let herself be taken. She could not recall his name. Frankie, Funzie, Petey, Sal—what did it matter? They were all preening, back-slapping show-offs; she could seldom even tell who were friends and who were enemies.

After a moment Nicky wagged the gun toward Al. "So who's this other asshole?"

Katy stayed silent. So did Al. Squid reached across and slammed the butt of his gun into the tall man's solar plexus. Fifi tried to nip his hand. "Answer the fucking question."

Al had a hard time getting his breath to hook up with his vocal cords. Weakly, he managed, "Name's Al Tuschman."

Squid's eyes pinwheeled. "*Big* Al Tuschman, any chance?"

"Wit' a license plate that says so?" put in Chop.

"Yeah," admitted the furniture salesman.

"I tol' ya!" Chop insisted.

"Shut up," said Nicky Scotto. "Let it go, already." To Katy he said, "But ya didn't come here wit' this asshole, did ya? Ya came here wit' the real Big Al."

Katy said nothing. Chop wound slowly through the streets. Cats skulked along the curbs. Brightening streetlamps put orange starbursts on the windshield.

"So where the fuck is he?" Nicky said.

Katy kept quiet. She was not a traitor. For the last few days she'd worked hard at killing her old life, shedding the hurt parts that had inhabited that life; she didn't need to kill old boyfriends too.

Nicky Scotto sucked his teeth, said with confidence, "You're gonna tell us."

She didn't.

Nicky plucked his clothing and tried a different tack. "This new asshole—you like 'im? I mean, I get the feeling you and him are hangin' out together now."

Katy said nothing. Al soothed his quivering dog.

"Listen, Kitty—"

"Katy."

"Katy," Nicky said. "Lemme put this very simple. Someone named Big Al is gonna die tonight. It can be the other one, who frankly is a useless scumbag, or it can be this guy you seem to like. I'm givin' you the chance to decide. Take a minute. Think it over."

He produced a toothpick from a jacket pocket, chomped it. Chop drove. He loved to drive; he could drive all night.

Katy looked at Al. It was too dark to really see his eyes. She saw his pitted cheek, one corner of his mouth. She liked his face but she couldn't bring herself to speak.

Nicky got impatient. He said to Squid, "Show the lady we're sincere."

Squid licked his lips and reached his hot, damp arm around her back; the hollow of his armpit cupped her flank. The gun was in his hand and he pressed the muzzle into the soft place behind Al Tuschman's ear. Contextless, obscene, it dented the flesh, traced out the seam between the skull and jaw. She felt Al tighten, felt his breathing stall. Squid cocked the hammer. The click seemed very loud.

Her shoulders sagged. She said, "Okay, okay."

The gun stayed where it was.

"Last I know, he's at the Conch House."

Squid withdrew his arm. Nicky almost smiled. The toothpick danced between his teeth. He looked at Chop.

Chop said, "That sucks."

"Whatsa matter?"

"Can't grab 'im there," the driver said. "Big fancy busy place. Tons a people. Guards."

Nicky plucked at his itching trousers. Chop serenely made left turns, right turns. Al touched Katy's knee with a hand that wasn't steady.

After a silence, Squid's voice had the harsh, damp rasp of a kazoo. "So she brings 'im to us."

Nicky looked at him.

"Come on," he said. "Two days ago they were an item. Big tall sexy babe like this, she lures 'im down."

Katy closed her eyes, forced herself to inhale.

Nicky considered. "We do 'im there?"

"Too closed in," said Squid. "Grab 'im's all we do."

Chop turned in the direction of Duval Street.

Squid swallowed, then kept talking like Al and Katy weren't there. "We give 'er an hour. She doesn't bring 'im down, the new Romeo is dead. We're no worse off than now."

Al Tuschman held his dog against his stomach. The quiet residential streets turned garish as they neared Duval. Neon flashed; the humid air took on blue and orange grains. Chop wove among mopeds and bicycles and pedicabs until he found the Conch House's garage.

He pulled in between a low ceiling and an oily concrete floor under evil, maddening fluorescent lights. He passed up some open spaces, crawled along until he saw a dark gray Lincoln with a New York plate that said BIG AL.

"Sonofabitch," he muttered. He parked across an aisle and a couple of slots away. He lowered the windows and switched off the engine. The air stank of exhaust.

With the motor off it was ungodly still. Nicky pushed back his sleeve and checked his watch. He spoke to Katy but pointed his gun at Al. "Ya got an hour, sweetheart. Smile pretty."

She kissed Al Tuschman on the cheek and climbed out of the car.

34

Katy was still wearing her pink shorts and lime-green top and high-heeled sandals, and the concrete floor felt very hard against her feet.

She walked stiffly to the elevator and tried to clear her head. She knew some things she wished she didn't know. She knew that thugs were liars, that there was not the slightest guarantee that she and Tusch would go free if she produced Big Al. She knew, as well, that she could probably escape, alone. Men like this—the truth was that, for all the jealousy and posing, women didn't matter to them; their deepest passions—hate, revenge, a pathetic need to be respected—were reserved for one another. With lack of regard came an insulting form of safety; she knew that she could simply disappear. And she knew she wouldn't do it.

She rode up to the top guest floor, approached the suite she'd shared with Big Al Marracotta. She tried to practice what she would say to him, but no words would come; there was nothing to rehearse. He would want to touch her, of course, reassert his claim. She shivered at the thought. She paused a moment at the door, then knocked.

There was no answer. She knocked again. Hearing silence in return, she bit her lip and pictured him at the rooftop bar. Pictured him with such intensity as to put him there, because, if he wasn't, there was no way she'd find him in an hour. She went back to the elevator.

. It was crowded on the rooftop. Smoke swirled. A piano player labored bravely against the giggling and the clank of ice and the whirring of the blenders. Katy, a woman alone in pink shorts and heels, pushed through the clustered bodies at the bar; a hand brushed against her buttocks. She broke through to the rank of small tables that edged the room, that owned the pricey windows. Waitresses careened with endless trays of fritters. Couples drank from salted glasses. And there, at a dim table in the corner, a sweating silver bucket poised in front of him, sat Big Al Marracotta by himself.

Katy, unseen, studied him a moment before she approached. He looked not just small but diminished, shrunken, like something revisited from childhood. His helmet of hair seemed unnatural, puppetlike. There was a hint of the primitive and stupid in the sensual looseness of his mouth. She braced herself and moved toward him.

He looked up from his glass and saw her when she was several steps away. The distance gave him time to select a pose. He was beaten down, defeated, and if he let it show he might know the sweetness of being comforted. But no way would he let it show. He stretched his neck inside his collar, stuck out his stubby chin.

"'Lo, Al," Katy said.

He turned his head way up to look at her. "You're back." He was surprised and yet it sounded smug.

"Ask me to sit down?"

He gestured toward a chair. "Where ya been?"

Sitting, she said, "Needed some time alone. You shouldn't have hit me, Al."

He might have said he was sorry. He *was* sorry. He said, "Didja come here to start another argument?"

She glanced at the champagne bottle. Big Al gestured for a waitress to bring another glass.

"I came," she said, "to see if maybe we should try again." She crossed her long legs. The edge of the tablecloth touched her skin just above the knee.

Al felt a twinge in his pants. He looked away like he was giving the proposition careful thought. He'd told himself he was through with Katy, especially when it seemed that she was through with him. Besides, without the market, who knew if he could even afford her anymore? But in the meantime she was tall, she was young, she was here.

The waitress brought a glass and poured for both of them. To Katy's relief, that drained the bottle.

She let Big Al play hard to get. She put her hand on his wrist. "I have an idea," she said. "Let's go someplace new, forget about what happened here, start fresh. A couple days in South Beach, maybe. Whaddya say?"

Big Al pursed his lips. He was struggling up from dismal depths, and the only way he knew to climb was to step on someone else. He said, "So ya realized when ya had it good."

Katy tried hard not to wince, used her glass to hide her face. "Yeah, Al. I realized."

He tipped his flute up to his sloppy lips, tapped out a final drop, pretended that he'd come to a decision. "Okay," he said. "Let's go downstairs."

She pictured the giant bed, smelled again the rank sheets and sour pillows. She turned coy to mask a sudden panic. "Okay," she said, "but just to pack."

"Right. Whatever. Sure."

"I mean it, Al. I don't wanna be here anymore."

He gestured for his tab and signed it. They rose and moved through the crowd toward the elevator. People looked at them— the slick and cocksure guy with the tall and chesty babe—and Big Al Marracotta felt almost back on top again.

Downstairs in the stifling and hellishly lit garage, Nicky Scotto plucked his sleeve and checked his watch. "Three quarters of an hour gone," he said. "The bitch ain't comin' back."

In the rear seat of the Jag, Squid Berman swiveled toward Al Tuschman. "Guess you didn't impress her much."

Al said nothing, petted his dog. He was very afraid but as time wore on and adrenaline subsided, his fear lost its jagged edge and became a smooth, round weight that was simply there, a background noise. Tentatively resigned, he found himself thinking almost calmly of morbid, dreadful things. What would become of Fifi if he got killed? Would she end up in some adoption agency full of horny, uncouth mutts in cages floored with filthy shredded newsprint? What about Moe Kleiman? Corny, generous old Moe—would he somehow blame himself?

And while he was on guilt, he felt terribly guilty about Katy. She'd drawn the tougher card by far. While he just sat here quietly communing with his cowardice, she was out there, acting, scheming in the face of her fear. Let the thugs say what they wanted; Al didn't for an instant doubt that she was trying her best to ransom him. That's who she was—a person who would try her best. But what if she just couldn't pull it off? What would a maniac like Big Al do if he realized she was trying to betray him? That was a question that made the background noise of Al Tuschman's fear rise again to a hideous jangle.

Minutes passed. Making chitchat, Nicky Scotto said to Chop, "So we ain't got Al but we got a place?"

Chop's eyes flicked to the rearview mirror before he answered. "Perfect place," he said. "Scoped it out this afternoon."

There was a silence.

Squid said to Nicky, "Ain't you hot, that suit on?"

Nicky didn't answer that, just plucked at the hated fabric and checked his watch again. "Ten minutes," he said. "Bitch ain't comin' back."

35

Big Al Marracotta's hands were groping toward Katy's breasts before the door had even closed behind them.

She seized his wrists, labored mightily to keep some playfulness in her voice. "Later," she said. "We're packing. We're going. Right?"

"What's the hurry?" said Big Al. He freed his hands and grabbed her hips and made lewd wiggles with his tongue.

Katy realized something in that instant. Realized that not only did he repulse her now, he'd repulsed her from the start, and that had been part of the appeal. Crazy, but no more.

She spun away, moved toward the stand that held her suitcase. Her breath caught when she saw the violence Big Al had wrought against her things, the slashed and sundered bras and panties and stockings. "Jesus," she said. "I guess you were pretty mad at me."

For one second he looked sheepish, then seemed stupidly proud of himself and of his rage. "Yeah," he said. "Pretty mad. Blind mad. Mad enough for anything."

Fright climbed up her throat with a taste of salt and iron. She managed something like a smile, said, "Guess you'll have to buy me some new things up in South Beach."

He liked that, as she knew he would. Made him feel like a sport. He licked his lips as he pictured her modeling a fresh batch of cheesy lingerie. He glanced over at the bags of sex toys. "Got some goodies to bring along."

She tried her best to look intrigued. "Sooner we get on the road . . ."

He leered at her, and ran a hand across his crotch, and moved off to the bathroom.

Katy lunged to the armoire, started stuffing clothes into Big Al's luggage. Cabana sets, black shirts, expensive shoes. Desperation made her wildly efficient. She went to the phone and called down to the kennel. Even moved the bags of sex toys toward the door. By the time Al Marracotta had peed and put himself away and combed his helmet of salt-and-pepper hair, all that was left to do was to gather up cosmetics. She swept tubes and bottles from the counter and announced that they were ready.

"The dog?" he said.

"They're getting him."

Not one to carry his own bags or retrieve his own car, Big Al Marracotta said, "Didja call a bellman? A valet?"

"They're all backed up," she lied. "Like half an hour. Come on, I'll carry stuff."

She bent to lift his suitcase. He put his hand on her flexing ass. "Why so anxious, babe?"

She bit her lip and forced her hips to move against his hand. "Come on, Al. Different place, different bed. Come on."

She moved off toward the door. He followed. It seemed to take forever for the elevator to arrive.

Nicky Scotto checked his watch then pointed his gun at Alan Tuschman's chest. "Ah, shit," he said. "Looks like we gotta kill ya."

Al stroked his dog and tried not to tremble. He thought he'd show himself that much, at least—get through this without quaking or crying or wetting his pants.

"Nothin' personal," Nicky went on. "Y'unnerstand, we don't follow through, people lose respect."

Chop made a somewhat sympathetic sound. "All over a stupid license plate. A stupid nickname."

"Wit' all the other nicknames you mighta had," put in Squid. "Knucklehead. Limpdick . . ."

Fifty yards away, the chrome doors of the elevator opened.

The rottweiler came out first. Penned in much too long, it strained at its leash, strained so hard it choked itself and wheezed.

The waiting killers heard the wheezing and the tick of paws against the oily cement floor. They looked up through the sickly bluish light, and in a moment they saw Katy, listing slightly on her high-heeled shoes as she balanced a fat suitcase, and Al Marracotta, rearing back against the weight of the leash, a pair of shopping bags sagging in his other hand.

A vindicated Nicky Scotto whispered, "Ya see? Ya see! Little guy. Big dog. Let's go."

Low and silent, he slipped out of the Jag, Squid Berman right behind. Squatting down between two cars, they readied their pieces as the footsteps drew closer. They held their breath and fixed their gazes on the vanity plate at the rear end of the Lincoln.

Big Al finally stood next to it. He put the shopping bags down on the cement and fished in his pocket for a key. He fumbled with the key, then had some trouble fitting it to the lock. He rubbed his eyes and started over. Everything seemed to be taking an unnaturally long time. At last the trunk swung open. He bent to put in the bags.

That's when Squid and Nicky came springing toward his rumpled, helpless back.

"Get your fuckin' hands up, Al!" said Scotto.

Katy dropped the suitcase, stepped aside fast.

By reflex, not yet knowing who it was that had the drop on him, the little mobster did as he was told. The leash fell from his hand. The restless but simple rottweiler, paralyzed by sudden freedom, sat down on the floor and let its tongue hang out. Squid Berman bounded close to Al, frisked him from his armpits to his groin.

"Now turn around," said Nicky.

Big Al pivoted, and when he saw his colleague from New York, he was a little afraid and quite pissed off, but mostly he was just confused. His confusion, like morning clouds, burned off one layer at a time, and the first thing he understood was that Katy, with her teasing talk of fresh beds, fresh lingerie, had set him up. He looked at her. "You fucking cunt."

She felt bad for him in spite of everything. Felt bad for his wife and kids, who probably thought he was an okay guy. She couldn't meet his eyes.

But Big Al couldn't figure out what Nicky Scotto wanted from him. Their little contest was over. He'd lost; Nicky had won. He said to his enemy, "Why the fuck—?"

A long moment's mayhem stifled his question.

Fifi had grown quiveringly alert in her master's lap. She smelled danger and the rottweiler. In whatever canine way she understood the battle, she was determined to do her part. She dug her paws into Al Tuschman's crotch and, before he could restrain her, she propelled herself out the Jaguar's open window.

Paws skidding on the slippery cement, she charged at Ripper, furiously yipping all the while. The chickenhearted rottweiler half stood up, retreating slowly, quailing. Then it made an epic blunder and turned its back. Beneath the russet bull's-eye of its ass, its showy testicles dangled and swayed, the right one lower than the left. Fifi made a mighty leap and grabbed them in her teeth.

The big dog howled and yelped and spun in tight and anguished circles. The little dog hung on, fur flying backward, legs and tail streaming out behind as though distended by the motion of some insane amusement-park ride. Ripper's scrotum stretched like pizza dough; Fifi flapped like laundry in a gale. Finally she loosed her grip, went scuttling across the floor. Ripper, whimpering and bloodied, ran limping for the exit.

Big Al Marracotta, hands still in the air, said, "Jesus Christ! My dog!"

"You don't need 'im anymore," said Nicky Scotto. "We're goin' for a ride."

Al tried to keep the terror out of his voice. "Nicky, come on. You got the market—"

"You're giving it ta me?" said the man with the gun. "That's very nice."

"Come on, don't kid around. I talked ta Tony. I know what's what."

Now it was Nicky who was a little bit confused. He labored not to let it show.

"It's yours," Big Al went on. "Fair enough. I ain't happy, but congratulations."

There was a pause. The lights buzzed. Drunken street noise filtered in. Katy sidled farther away from her former boyfriend.

Nicky said, "Tony tol' ya this?"

"Yesterday. Said the market goes back ta Nicky. Said my time was like a tryout. I'm pissed but that's life."

Scotto pursed his lips, scratched his eyebrow, pulled his ear. For an instant he lowered his gun. Then he said, "Nice try, Al. Had me goin' for a second. But don'tcha think Tony woulda called me first?"

Weakly, Big Al Marracotta said, "He didn't?"

"You got balls," said Nicky. "I give ya that."

Using his pistol to point the way, he gestured toward the Jag. Big Al didn't budge. Squid moved close and shoved him along.

Chop pulled the lever that released the trunk. It yawned open slowly, like the mouth of a whale. Nicky said, "Hop in."

Big Al said, "Please. You're makin' a mistake. Call Tony—"

Squid raised his gun butt, gave him one brisk hack where the spine ended and the skull began, and caught him neatly by the armpits as he sagged. He muscled him into the trunk and slammed the lid on top of him.

Nicky turned his gun toward Katy and ordered her into the car.

She stood where she was. Trying to sound firm, trying to convince him with her righteous certainty, she said, "You got your guy. We can go now, right?"

"Sorry, sister. Job ain't finished yet."

"But you said—"

Squid was moving toward her across the oily floor. He grabbed her almost gently by the elbow.

Nicky interrupted her. "What I said is that I don't like witnesses. Get inna fucking car."

Ushered by Squid, dizzy on her high shoes, she slid into the backseat once again, allowed herself a shudder and a groan as she nestled next to Tusch. Fifi bounded onto his lap, licked their joined hands.

"That's quite a dog you got," said Squid.

Chop drove off slowly through the scattered drops of blood that the rottweiler had left behind.

36

Halfway to Stock Island, Big Al Marracotta woke up in the trunk.

It was pitch dark in there, with just a small supply of viscous air that smelled of grease and rubber. The tires were loud as their treads sucked at the pavement, and he bounced with every seam in the road. Potholes sent him flying against the underside of the lid. He curled up and cradled his head and wondered if it was absolutely certain that he was being taken to die.

In the passenger compartment, things were not much cheerier. For a while no one spoke. Al and Katy leaned against each other, their flanks growing very warm where they touched. The heroic shih tzu perched proudly on her master's lap as a few hideous miles of U.S. 1 slipped past in what was now full night. There was the glare of fast-food joints and desperate strip malls, crappy motels shilled by giant signs that throbbed like boils. Nicky Scotto plucked at his pants and wondered if, with Big Al gone and the fish market solidly his, he might ease back into wearing decent suits.

Chop approached the little bridge at Cow Key Channel. Squid pointed to a hollow on the far side of the road. "That's where we picked up your stupid license plate," he told Al Tuschman. "Tailed you all the way to your hotel. You didn't notice nothin'."

No, the furniture salesman admitted to himself, he hadn't. But why would he have? He wasn't a criminal, didn't have violent enemies, didn't have to live life looking back across his shoulder. He'd arrived in Key West, just a few short days ago, as one more average schmo with average hopes for his vacation. Get a tan, maybe meet a woman. Step, however briefly, however meekly, outside the self he was by habit, and go home with life enriched by a memory or two. Modest expectations; sane expectations. Why would he have noticed, or believed, that two maniacs suddenly were out to get him?

They drove past tattoo parlors, liquor stores.

In the trunk, Big Al Marracotta bounced and rolled, and tried to avoid admitting he was terrified by getting more and more pissed off. Disagreements happened; guys got iced. He accepted this, except when it was happening to him. Now it all seemed senseless and unjust. Why was he getting killed? Because that putz Benny Franco got himself indicted? Because Tony Eggs didn't make a phone call?

Or was it even crazier and more infuriating than that? Was he getting killed because he took vacation? This was the price of a goddamn week away from work? Or was it that he took vacation with a no-good, ingrate tramp who sold him out?

Baffled and furious, he bounced, he tumbled, and gradually he realized that he was running out of air. He had to pull hard from the bottom of his lungs to inhale; he smelled his own stale breath going into him again. In the blackness of the trunk, he felt a sudden excruciating loneliness, previewed the unspeakable remove of being dead, and the helpless and humiliating sorrow of it only made him madder. He swore to himself a solemn pledge: if he was going down because of all this unfair craziness, these betrayals and these blunders, he wasn't going down alone.

Curled up, panting, he reached toward his ankle. He felt for the slender knife that Squid's hurried frisking hadn't found. One knife against three guns—there was no chance he could save himself. Yet there was a certain spiteful comfort in knowing there was still somebody weaker he could hurt. Pulling the weapon smoothly from its leather sheath, he tucked it up his sleeve between the bounces of the car. He pulled hard at the rank and thinning air, and took a final nasty pleasure from figuring how he might slash and tear the woman who had turned on him.

Chop turned off the highway at MacDonald Avenue, then wound through streets of deepening dreariness.

Dim and secret bars gave way to crowded plots of rusting trailers lifted up on cinder blocks; the trailers yielded to a precinct of windowless garages housing auto-body and machine shops. Where the asphalt ended and the road became humped gravel dotted with deep foul puddles that would never dry, there were random shacks with kinked and crumpled metal roofs, their grassless yards littered with splotched banana leaves and decomposing fronds. Streetlamps grew sparse; they wavered in uncertain, percolating ground that was only inches higher than the ocean. There was a smell in the air of sea corrupted, a salty stink like that of anchovies kept too long in the tin.

Chop serenely drove; the Jaguar clattered over stones. Dead ahead, inexplicably standing sentinel in the middle of the street, there was what appeared to be an ancient tollbooth. It leaned on rotting stakes; boards were missing from its wooden flanks; there was no glass in its windows.

On closer inspection, it proved to be the box office for a long-abandoned drive-in theater.

Beyond the tiny building, bathed in wan and opalescent moonlight, stretched the ghostly parking field. Low concentric mounds built up of shells and bits of coral lifted vanished cars to perfect viewpoints. The posts that had held the scratchy speakers poked up crooked from the contours. The screen itself—its paint long seared away by sun and salt, its plywood face splintery and scarred—loomed patiently, waiting for the inevitable wind that would send it crashing down.

Chop rode the mounds like waves, finally broke the silence. "Good place, huh?" he said to Nicky.

"Beautiful."

Gasping in the trunk, Big Al Marracotta bounced and rolled with every hump.

The driver headed for what once had been the snack bar, a fragrant place of Milk Duds and malteds and soggy burgers wrapped in foil. Boarded and imploding now, it was only something to hide behind. Chop pulled up near it and switched the engine off.

27

They climbed out of the car.

Nicky plucked at his damp and hated suit. Squid twisted his torso, stretched his bandy muscles. Chop halfheartedly produced a gun, but seemed to wish he was still behind the wheel.

Fifi jogged in little circles, then paused to sniff the seam where the snack bar met the ground, detected memories, perhaps, of ancient popcorn, archaic franks. Katy rose up tall on her high-heeled sandals. The night air was still warm against her legs; she concentrated on the feeling. Al Tuschman stood close to her and looked up at the rotting, tilting movie screen backed by a spray of starlight. Drive-ins had been big in Jersey. He remembered going in pajamas as a little kid. Life seemed very safe then.

Nicky and Squid trained their pistols on the Jaguar's trunk. Chop flipped a lever and the lid yawned open.

Moonlight wedged in, and Big Al Marracotta squinted at the sudden brightness, sucked greedily at the rush of salty air. Nicky said to him, "Get up."

It wasn't that easy. His legs had cramped, his blood grown grainy and stagnant. He rocked and strained, flopped like a fish on the beach. Eventually he was sitting on the trunk's sharp lip, his small feet not reaching to the ground. He looked straight at Nicky's gun and said, "You really don't have to do this."

"Hey," said Nicky, "you've seen my cards. Gotta finish out the hand."

Big Al bit his lip, looked around. Absently, he said, "Fuckin' drive-in? Ain't seen one a these in years."

No one joined the conversation.

Big Al stared over at Katy, measured the distance between them. Twelve, fifteen feet. She was standing next to the big guy with the curly hair. Not touching, but very close. He said to her, "So you're wit' this asshole now?"

Katy didn't answer that.

Big Al said, "Boom—just like that. After all I done for you."

Katy said nothing.

Big Al shook his head. And lightly shook his arm, so that the tip of his knife rested against the heel of his hand just at the edge of his cuff. "Well," he said, "win some, lose some. No hard feelings."

He looked down a moment then said to Nicky, "Bitch cost me a lot. Still, good girlfriend, lotta ways. Mind I kiss her goo'bye?"

Nicky seemed bleakly amused by the show of gallows sentiment. It was all the same to him. They were both dead people anyway. He just shrugged by way of answer.

Big Al eased down from the trunk. His weird hair gleamed like plastic in the moonlight. Shells and knobs of coral crunched beneath his shoes. Slowly and deliberately, he turned his back on the men with guns and shuffled toward his former girlfriend. For a moment that boy-devil grin was on his face, then his lips got hard and flat. Katy leaned backward on her shoes but couldn't get her feet to move.

He approached without hurry. The ground crackled beneath him. He turned his wrist just slightly so that it faced away from Nicky and Chop and Squid. When he was a single stride from Katy, he twitched his hand and the knife blade slid down across his palm and he caught the hot handle in his fingers.

Alan Tuschman saw the blade glint in the moonlight, saw Big Al Marracotta crouch ever so slightly to turn his next step into a thrusting lunge.

He had no time to think. He had only that fraction of a heartbeat in which the brave man acted while the phony hero postured, and bargained with his nerve, and thereby lost the moment. Al Tuschman didn't hesitate.

Stomping fear, throttling caution, he threw himself in front of Katy, across the path of Big Al Marracotta's jabbing blade. He grabbed at his namesake's flailing arm but didn't catch it cleanly; Marracotta jerked his hand free and stabbed up toward Tuschman's neck. The salesman deflected the thrust, but the knife slashed past his shoulder. He felt it cut his shirt and slice his skin and bit through to the yielding flesh. With the ooze of blood came less pain than an ecstatic charge, a hectic self-forgiveness of past shirkings and doubts and fallings-short.

Wounded and wildly heedless, Al Tuschman bulled straight at the man with the knife. Marracotta thrust again. The tall man seized his pumping arm; the knife flashed and wiggled like a snake. For a long moment the two Als pressed against each other in a dreadful stalemate, then the mobster lost his footing on the loose and chalky gravel, and they both went tumbling to the mounded ground.

Fifi circled and barked and nipped at Marracotta's ankles. Amid the tumult, no one noticed that Squid had slipped away. No one paid attention to the grinding start-up of a different engine.

Al Tuschman scrambled flat on top of Big Al Marracotta, slugged him awkwardly across the chin. The short man kneed him in the groin and rolled him over and strained to lift the arm that held the knife. The salesman kept a hand clamped around the mobster's wrist and struggled to hang on. Marracotta lifted, grunted . . . and Tuschman suddenly let go, bucking and shoving as Marracotta's unsprung arm flew up and wrecked his balance. The little gangster tipped over and crashed onto his side. The impact of his landing shook the knife out of his hand; it skated over shells and coral for half a dozen feet.

Big Al went crawling after it. He was about to grab it when a pair of long bare legs moved in to block his path.

Katy Sansone lifted up a high-heeled sandal and kicked him

in the face. He saw the shoe hurtling toward him and then he felt his nose cave in, spiky shards intruding on his passages. Like a half-crushed bug he tried to keep on crawling, swimming toward the knife, but Al Tuschman had him by the feet, pulled him back across the lacerating shells.

The desperate and preposterous tug-of-war went on for several seconds, then Nicky Scotto sauntered over and, with a wagging pistol, called it off. Dryly, he said, "Amateur wrestling. Tag-team. Very entertaining."

Big Al lifted his neck and rolled his eyes way up like in a painting of a saint, saw Nicky's gun poised not far above his head. He tried to speak but blood and mucus had pooled in his throat and for the moment he could only gurgle. He kicked his legs and made a reflexive attempt at standing.

Nicky cocked the hammer of his pistol. "Don't bother getting up," he said. "You'll only fall back down again."

That's when the truck came tearing around the back side of the snack bar.

It whined and roared, its tires spitting gravel out behind as it rocked on the uneven ground. Glowing softly in the moonlight, the writing on the trailer said LOWER KEYS SEAFOOD COMPANY— EAT FISH LIVE LONGER. Through a glaring silver starburst on the windshield, Squid could just barely be seen, manically grinning, spasmodically swallowing. He drove straight at Big Al.

"Jesus Christ," said Nicky, as everybody scattered.

Al Marracotta, his back to the screaming vehicle, crawled and reared and scrabbled to his knees but was flattened by the fender and pounded like a cutlet by the left front tire. It crushed his ribs; the doubled rear wheels wrung his innards out like sponges, made them into paste. He twitched once like a shocked frog, and after that was still.

The truck's momentum carried it another fifty yards. It came to a skidding halt on the coral rubble and slowly turned around. Squid paused a moment then revved it high in first, slammed it into second.

"The motherfucker's crazy," Nicky said, though it would be another moment before he realized that the seafood truck was coming back for him.

He didn't realize that until the truck had veered so that its hood ornament was pointing squarely at his face. Disbelieving still, he yelled out, "Hey!" And when the truck did not change course, he raised his gun and shot the windshield out.

Squid Berman, hunkered down beneath the dashboard, reveled in the spray of broken glass.

Nicky Scotto fired again, this time murdering the radiator, and then he started running, his stiff, cheap jacket flying out behind. He took off over humps and mounds, past headless speaker posts sprouting bouquets of disconnected wires. Squid dogged him like a cowboy, pivoting and leaning, motor whining like a whinnying horse. Nicky ran along the contour of a mound, seemed for a deranged moment to be racing across the drive-in screen. Finally, legs heavy, breath failing, he turned around to fire once more. The bullet exploded a sideview mirror, but after that, winded and dispirited, the doomed man could hardly do more than jog.

The truck caught up with him but failed to run him over. It somehow lifted him behind the knees and waffled him against the grille, broken but alive. A disembodied hand raised up grotesquely, wagged a moonlit gun above the level of the hood. Squid Berman floored the truck and headed for a speaker post, used Nicky Scotto's body as a ram to knock it down. The pistol went off skyward as his back was snapped and his lifeless body rolled in its horrendous suit down a hump of shells and coral.

38

"*I wasn't afraid!* I wasn't afraid!" Al Tuschman had said to Katy in the moment before his knees had buckled and he'd crumpled slowly to the ground.

He sat there now, his back against the Jag, his eyes tracking with a dreadful fascination the homicides by seafood truck. Katy sat near him, dabbing his cut shoulder with a hankie. Fifi smelled her master's precious blood; full of worry and compassion, she wouldn't stop licking his hand.

Chop nonchalantly kept his gun pointed at the captives as he watched his partner run people down.

Then Squid drove back across the humps and mounds and screeched to a stop half a dozen feet away. The truck's windshield consisted now of several snaggled shards quaking in the frame. Antifreeze was dribbling from below and the engine was already smoking. The driver jumped down from the cab, arms twitching, tongue busy at the corners of his mouth.

"Nice work," Chop said to him.

Modest and not completely satisfied, Squid said only, "Aawh."

He did a little pirouette, then pulled his pistol from the waistband of his pants, and for a few moments he paced intently back and forth in front of Al and Katy. Moonlight rained down and a smell of damp rubber rose up from Big Al Marracotta's corpse. Whenever Squid changed the direction of his pacing, his feet broke some seashells and they made a crispy sound.

Finally he paused, leaned low before his captives, and barked right into their faces, "I fucking hate to make mistakes!"

He sprang into motion once again, and added, "It's like noisy, cockeyed, out of tune. Depressing. Ya see what I'm saying?"

Cautiously, Al and Katy nodded.

"Coulda been a masterpiece, this job," the bandy man continued. "Had everything. Theme. Shape. Room ta improvise. Instead I hadda backtrack and erase. And now I got these extra pieces."

"Extra pieces?" said Al Tuschman.

"You, numbnuts."

A puff of breeze made the tilting movie screen groan on its moldy pilings. Squid kept on pacing and Fifi kept swiveling her head to track him. After a time he stopped again, crouched down, and put the muzzle of the gun very close to Alan Tuschman's forehead. He said, "Lemme ask you a fairly important question. Tell me what you did tonight."

A little cross-eyed, Al said, "Huh?"

"You deaf?"

Katy said, "We checked out of our hotel. Rented a car. Drove up to South Beach."

"Meet anyone? See anything unusual along the way?"

"Nobody," said Katy. "Nothing."

"Nothing at all," Al Tuschman blithely said.

"Then how'dya cut your shoulder?"

"Umm . . ."

"Lover's quarrel," Katy said. "Nobody's business."

Squid considered that a moment, then he started pacing once again. In his pacing was the torment of the artist before a canvas that simply would not come together. Sighing, he said at last, "Look, it bothers me ta have ta kill ya. But come on. After what you saw? Nicky woulda took you out. Big Al woulda took you out."

"And look where it got them," said Katy.

"Not the point," said Squid.

He did his anguished laps. Chop, impatient, started slapping his gun against his other palm. Al Tuschman's mouth went very dry.

After a moment Katy said, "But we're the ones who did it."

Squid said, "What?"

"Mind if I get up?"

She unfolded very smoothly, brushed coral dust from the backs of her legs. Slowly and deliberately, she moved toward the truck. With Squid right behind her, she climbed into the driver's seat, firmly wrapped her hands around the steering wheel. Then, through the vacant windshield, she called out, "Tusch—pick up the knife."

The salesman rose on shaky legs, found Big Al Marracotta's blade against the pale, rough stones, squeezed the handle in his palm.

Katy said to Squid. "Nice clear fingerprints." She pointed to Al's bloody shoulder. "Signs of a struggle. Stormy history with the deceased. Love triangle gone wrong."

Squid did a crunching pirouette and thought it over. Then he jerked a thumb in the direction of the other corpse. "And Nicky?"

"Showed up in the wrong place at the wrong time."

Squid scrunched up his mouth. "Sloppy."

"Hey," said Katy, "jobs sometimes have extra pieces, right? Besides, it's still easier to believe than what really happened."

"That's a point," the bandy man conceded.

"I ran these guys over," she said. "To save Tusch, who was fighting with the knife. Are we going to the cops?"

Squid pawed the ground, swallowed deeply, pulled his ear. Finally he looked at Chop.

Chop rubbed his stumpy neck, said, "I got nothin' against these people, long as they don't get stupid."

Squid licked extra wetness from the corners of his mouth, said to no one in particular, "Would blow the symmetry, we waste the extra pieces."

laurence shames

"Wouldn't be symmetrical at all," said Alan Tuschman. "Would be like both end tables on the same side of the couch."

Squid told him to shut up.

Feigning confidence, Katy got down from the truck. She tried not to let it show that she was trembling as she offered Squid her back.

But he'd made up his mind. He didn't shoot her. He made a moist noise protesting all the world's rough edges, all the bumps and snags that mocked perfection. Then he put the pistol in the waistband of his pants and started walking toward the Jag.

Chop seemed to remember something then. He opened the passenger door, reached into the glove box, and retrieved a crumpled piece of paper. He handed it to Al.

Al couldn't read it in the moonlight.

"Pick-up order from Sun Motors," Chop explained. "Driver's signature. Proves they came and got your car. They had it, they lost it, they owe you a new one. . . . Myself, I think it looks better in navy."

He went around to the driver's side, climbed in, and started up the engine. Squid settled into the passenger seat and propped a bandy forearm on the window frame. "And get a different license plate," he said.

Al nodded that he would, then moved close to Katy in the moonlight. The shih tzu wiggled among their ankles and wagged its tail. They looked at the car that was about to pull away, and the tableau, in some unlikely manner, suggested a reluctant parting of old friends.

Almost sheepishly, Squid said, "Hey, no hard feelings, huh? Sorry ta fuck up your vacation."

"Ya didn't fuck it up," Al Tuschman volunteered.

"I didn't?" In spite of himself he sounded disappointed.

"Just made it sort of different," the salesman from New Jersey said. He took Katy's hand, took it in the serious way, with all the fingers interlinked. "Made it more a mission, kind of."

EPILOGUE

"Poor Nicky," said Donnie Falcone as he hung up the pay phone in the social club on Prince Street and moved languidly back toward the table he was sharing with his uncle and their dying *consigliere.*

"Stupid Nicky," Tony Eggs corrected.

Donnie came forth with a rueful little laugh, gave his chin a squeeze. "Yeah, not the sharpest knife inna drawer," he said. "Pretty easy ta string 'im along." He sat down and reclaimed his glass of anisette. *"Salud."*

Salud. Health. Carlo Ganucci's eyeballs were bright yellow and the skin of his neck was blue. Tony Eggs had kidney stones and his teeth were loose in their sockets. The two old men joined in the toast.

Shaking his head, Donnie went on. "Right from the start, I knew that all I hadda do was give 'im advice th' opposite a what I really wanted. I tell 'im don't even think about takin' the market back, right away that's all he thinks about."

"He wanted that job bad," Tony Eggs put in, and could not help smiling, showing mottled gums. "Ya shoulda seen the dumb fuck stomp his suit."

"I tell 'im don't even think about goin' ta Flahda," Donnie said, "right away I know damn well he's goin'."

Carlo Ganucci roused himself to say, "But howd'ya know who he was workin' wit' down 'ere?"

Donnie laughed. "I asked him. Casual like. He tells me guy who does cars in Hialeah. Then it's no problem gettin' in touch through our people in Miami."

Tony Eggs tugged at the fraying collar of his plain white shirt. "An' once ya got in touch," he said, "ya knew how ta get the best work from these people. One guy likes ta hijack trucks, ya let 'im grab a truck. Th' other guy has this thing, he wants ta do the job wit' seafood, ya let 'im do it wit' seafood. Ya motivated 'em good."

"Didn't hurt," said Donnie, "that I paid 'em double what Nicky was."

"Aaw, the money's overrated," Tony said. "Point is, you're a natural manager. This is why you're gonna do brilliant wit' the market."

Donnie made an attempt at sounding humble. "I'll try, *zio*. Ya know I'll do my best."

Tony Eggs patted his beloved nephew's cheek. "An' 'iss way," he said, "no one can accuse me playin' favorites. I tried two other guys. My fault they turned out ta be assholes? My fault they took each other out? Am I right, or am I right, Carlo?"

The old *consigliere* smiled faintly at the intrigue. He blinked. It took him a long time to get his crinkled and translucent eyelids to roll back up again.

"But here's one thing I still don't get," Tony Eggs resumed. "I know ya worked a deal wit' our people inna Catskills ta get inta that kitchen . . . but howd'ya poison the clams?"

Donnie leaned in a little closer. "Raw chicken."

"Raw chicken?"

"Took a chicken," Donnie said. "Left it out a coupla days. Got that whaddyacallit, salmonella, going. Took a brush, stuck it up the chicken's ass, dabbed a little funky juice on all the clams. Simple."

The old boss shook his head admiringly, showed his long loose teeth. "Salmonella. Beautiful." His nephew was the right guy for the job. He had no doubt of it. He raised his glass to the fish market's new regime. *"Salud."*

"Salud."
"Salud."

Katy liked the car in powder blue, so powder blue it was. Looked smart with the gray velour upholstery that, Al knew from his swatchbooks, went for twenty-eight, thirty bucks a yard. It was noon when they drove it off the lot in Miami, and they headed straight for the causeway to the Beach, still deter-mined to have a day at least of real vacation.

They parked on Ocean Drive. Stylish cafés on one side of the road, the endless Atlantic on the other. Nothing to do but eat and stroll and gawk at people.

Katy unfolded smoothly, took a gulp of warm salt air. "Fi-nally," she said, "I feel like a regular tourist."

Al Tuschman leashed his dog and locked the car and looked back across his bandaged shoulder. No one seemed to be tailing him, no one fighting for his nickname or contesting the space he took up in the world. "Seems a little tame."

"Tame's okay," said Katy.

He thought about that, and about the life that he'd be going back to. The store, the diners, his garden apartment condo. "Yeah," he said. "I guess it is." He craned his neck at avenue and beach. "Eat or walk?"

"Eat."

They picked a nearby place for its mix of shade and sun, then settled into varnished wicker chairs that faced the sidewalk, or-dered drinks and looked absently, distractedly at menus. New lovers. There was everything to say and it was frightening to have a conversation. Chitchat could sound too easily like making plans; plans came too close to being promises. So they silently held hands and people-watched. Models went by with portfolios. Gym-boys sported cut-off shirts that showed their waffled abs.

After a while, Al got reckless. He'd been out of danger half a day and some element of risk was missing from his life. So he said to Katy, "What'll you do when you get back? About your apartment, stuff like that?"

She shrugged, pushed her big sunglasses a little higher on her nose. "Move out, I guess. Find another place, a job."

Al nodded. The nod was neutral, matter-of-fact, but behind it Al was communing with his newfound courage. The brave man didn't posture, didn't bargain. The brave man seized the moment. Blandly, looking half away, he said, "Ever spend much time in Jersey?"

Katy understood that this was not a promise, that no promise was being asked for in return. Still, for new lovers the entire world was wet cement; the lightest stepping left its print. She looked at Tusch but was saved from answering by the waiter's arrival with their lunch.

"Who's got the shore platter?" he asked.

He put it down in front of Al. Half a lobster with a single claw outstretched. Curls of calamari piled up on lettuce. Six clams laid out in a gleaming arc.

Al Tuschman looked at his new lover and just shook his head. "I can't believe I ordered that," he said.

About the Author

LAURENCE SHAMES is the author of six previous Key West novels: *Mangrove Squeeze, Virgin Heat, Tropical Depression, Sunburn, Scavenger Reef,* and *Florida Straits.* He is also the uncredited co-writer of the *New York Times* bestseller *Boss of Bosses.* He lives with his wife, Marilyn, in Key West, Florida.